EXILES

ALSO BY MASON COILE

William

A Novel

MASON COILE

G. P. Putnam's Sons
New York

PUTNAM
— EST. 1838 —
G. P. Putnam's Sons
Publishers Since 1838
An imprint of Penguin Random House LLC
1745 Broadway, New York, NY 10019
penguinrandomhouse.com

Book design by Laura K. Corless

Hardcover ISBN: 9780593851630
Ebook ISBN: 9780593851647

Printed in the United States of America
1st Printing

The authorized representative in the EU for product safety and compliance is
Penguin Random House Ireland, Morrison Chambers, 32 Nassau Street,
Dublin D02 YH68, Ireland, https://eu-contact.penguin.ie.

For my wife, Heidi

EXILES

The beeping won't stop.

The beeping is sound become pain.

The beeping is the pulse of eternity.

The beeping is what I deserve.

The beeping is waking me from the longest sleep of my life.

2

You look like a greasy sheet of used parchment paper."

This is Kang, crouched next to my pod as I pull myself up and spill my legs over the side.

"A weirdly specific image," I say. "But I'll take it, considering I went into this thing four months ago."

"How about me?"

"You mean how do you look?"

"Yeah."

"I'll tell you anything you want to hear if you turn off that noise."

"What?" He cocks his head like a dog listening for the distant call of his name. "You mean this?"

Kang reaches out his hand without looking and flicks a black button on the wall that looks exactly like twenty other black buttons around it. The beeping stops.

"They didn't warn us how long we'd have to listen to *that*," I say.

"They didn't warn us about most of the things that could actually go wrong."

"Really? It felt like Mission Leader was reciting from the *Bible of Terrifying Worst-Case Scenarios* for two years straight."

"That was just what they could *predict*. The interesting shit is going to be all the gruesome things they couldn't imagine."

"You seem excited about that."

Kang shrugs. "I guess I am."

"Why's that?"

"I think one of them is already happening."

o   o   o

What's the worst part of long-voyage space travel? There's no shortage of options. A bathroom the size of a mini-fridge that leaves you a permanent hunchback. Having to crawl through humming tubes that connect the barely larger "communals" so that it feels like you're living in a maze of MRIs. Masturbating in a sleep pod the dimensions of a coffin with one panel made of glass to ensure there's zero privacy to go along with the claustrophobia.

All strong contenders, no question. But my personal nominee would have to be the first crap after being juiced awake from extend-sleep. I could attempt a description of the experience but just thinking about it brings a stabbing pain in my hunchback.

And then there's what Mission Leader referenced in our training, in an even more ominous tone than when describing the effects of cosmic radiation poisoning, or roasting alive on atmospheric entry: "the interpersonal risks."

The *Valiant* was launched from beyond the aura of the Earth's blue glow seven months ago. It would've been a long time to be awake, twiddling your thumbs. The necessity for extend-sleep didn't come from concerns about our boredom, however, but from our potential to go apeshit in a ship that felt (and often smelled) like being inside a sardine can. And outside? Nothing but space. Thousands of people, a handful of nations, and several billions of dollars have gone into this mission. It would be a shame for it to fail because the crew decided to stick sporks in each other's throats just for a change of pace.

We know we were individually chosen at least in part for our skill sets, the practical things we can do: Blake is crew leader and pilot, Kang is the engineer, and I'm the medical officer. There's overlap in there too—I know enough that I could fly the landing pod if I had to. Probably. Kang's been taught how to amputate a gangrenous arm or leg, and Blake seems able to do just about anything.

Our skills weren't the only reason we were selected though. There were better, more experienced engineers and pilots and doctors among the thousand candidates that got cut. As a crew, the main test was whether we'd be able to keep the sporks down for the journey and, assuming safe arrival, minimize conflict for the remainder of our lives, aka the "breathing hours" we have left, as measured by the available oxygen inside the base's walls. *You need to get along,* as Mission Leader put it, her arms stacked like a pair of steel bars over her chest. And we do. We get along. Even if that's not exactly the same thing as liking each other.

We're going to Mars and never coming back.

If all goes according to plan, the three of us—the entirety of *Valiant*'s crew—will be the first humans to live and die on a planet other than Earth. A history-making triumph for some, a bleak honor for others. My own membership being with the latter camp. So why sign up? Why lie about being comfortable in small spaces, make up a story about dreaming of reaching the stars since I was a little girl, put up with the Mission Leader's physical and psychological abuse throughout the training and crew selection process?

I have no fucking idea.

I know it doesn't make sense, to come this far without a good reason. Which is why I haven't shared it with anyone—my crewmates or Mission Leader or the battery of psych quizmasters testing our resolve. Sometimes I think I've come all the way out here to find out.

∘ ∘ ∘

"You better follow me," Kang says, and then he's crawling into the tube that leads to Operations.

I'd asked him what he meant about something bad already happening, aware that he wasn't going to answer me, that he'd leave that for Blake to do. This may have been an adherence to protocol, though I strongly suspect that it's just another point on the Asshole Spectrum for Kang. Not that he's a bad guy, not an outright menace or anything. In fact, there's a lot about him to admire: loyalty, courage, a surprisingly goofy sense of humor. He's just kind of a dick. Low-range irritating in the way of an older brother, or at least what I imagine an older brother would be like if I had one.

Only child, parents both gone. It could be this "adult orphan" status even helped my candidacy. I sort of get it if it did. Here's what I don't get: Why they put the three of us, one woman and two men, all straight, together when we're not allowed to have sex. Maybe they evaluated the attraction levels between us and didn't see that worry ever coming up. Can they do that? I have no idea. But we had to take so many psych tests and sit through so many interactive scenarios, they probably know more about us than we do ourselves, including any undiscovered fetishes or erotic triggers.

Sex is where everything goes wrong, apparently. There aren't many elements more essential to achieving the *need to get along* goal than eliminating that particular complication. It would be important to know if jealousy might arise between Kang and Blake as we wait two years for the next half dozen "pioneers" to join us. Or maybe I might turn out to be the issue. Maybe I have a secret thing for one of them, or both, and sex this early in the mission— pregnancy being the main but far from only resulting problem—is strictly against protocol.

This is not a reproductive phase of our colonization, Mission Leader would remind me. She repeated this more than anything else. *You are initial base occupation only. The baby-making comes later—too late for you.*

Yet here I am, watching Kang scooch into the tube, reflecting not for the first time on how I would never date a man like him in a thousand years, but wouldn't mind fucking him in this hopeless bucket if the mission laws didn't forbid it.

See? There's got to be five whole seconds right there of me thinking about it. Wasted time. How did that inefficiency get through the tests?

I cleanse my mind of the dirtiest of dirty bits. Then I get down on my knees and follow Kang's ass into the tube's white glow.

3

Blake is waiting for us in Operations. His *Easily Distracted By Football* coffee mug is in the holder of the arm of his pilot's chair. He looks like a trucker to begin with, and never more so than from the pose he's in now, leaning back, squinting at us like signposts through a windshield. I notice the mug is empty. If he didn't have time to fill it with instant joe before calling us in here, right out of extend-sleep, there's got to be something truly pear-shaped going on.

Not that he tells us right away. Kang takes his chair next to him and I sit in mine across the cramped mess table. Blake sits up straight and places his hands on his knees but his brain's not here, kidnapped by intruding thoughts. It seems like someone will have to say something to bring him back, so I decide it'll be me.

"What's up, boss?"

"There's some irregularities on comms," he says, and immediately it's confirmed: this is serious. He only chooses words like that—*irregularities*—when he's trying to diminish the significance of a problem. Normally, when it's a situation he has in hand, he would be saying "There's some fuckups on comms."

"What kind?"

"At some point during our extend-sleep—we lost contact with Citadel."

Citadel being the name of the base awaiting our arrival. Citadel being our home on Mars.

"Is it our tech that's down, or the base's?"

"That's the odd part. Our tech looks to be good, and so is Citadel's."

"What's the problem then?"

"Nobody's answering at the other end."

"The worker bots?" Kang says.

"The logs indicate they were operational up until forty-two hours ago. Now they can't answer a call."

"They've got to know we're almost there," I say. "It's all they've been programmed to do. Get the base ready for us."

"They should be polishing the silverware," Kang says.

"I agree there isn't an obvious explanation. Every part of their mission has been accomplished, from all the indications I've seen. They're good machines," Blake says. "But now they've gone quiet."

We all go quiet too. Absorbing. Calling on the parts of our training intended to prevent us from freaking out when things go wrong. Controlled breathing. Staying solution focused. Refusing to be the weak link in the chain. Remembering why we're here. All of them helpful except the last one.

The three of us are equally aware what this news means, how jeopardizing it is to the mission—to our lives. We're puzzling out the work-arounds or justifications for calling everything off and heading home. We're also handling the turn of events in our own trademark ways.

Kang is moving his head from side to side in micro-shakes ostensibly meant only for himself. He takes bad luck personally. *Of course this shit is happening to* me. It's his way of managing anxiety by converting it into cosmic injustice. An unfair god he has no choice but to don his armor and face off against.

And then there's Blake.

He doesn't just look like any trucker. He looks like a trucker who went to Yale, which he, in fact, did. I'm fairly sure why he signed up, beyond the obvious motivations of a career military guy looking for a chance to leap up the rank ladder. He needed a new life after the one he had lined up was taken away. Marriage. Kids. Things he would've been good at, but never really got the chance to prove it. He was briefly married before his wife died. "Gone before we had a chance to empty the boxes in our first apartment." I asked, once, how she passed. "That's not for you," he said, sharp as a knifepoint between my ribs. I haven't gone close to asking again.

What I do know is that it rewired him beyond the usual ways that come with grief. In Blake's case, the takeaway was that fate saw him as unqualified for partnership or parenthood or any earthbound contentment. He was meant for the solitude of cramped pods, long silences, a journey as far from humanity as conceivable. This is how he put it to me, more or less, on the occasions when beer and Chivas eased it out of him.

"We're getting a message," Kang says.

We all know who it's going to be before her voice comes over the speakers: Mission Leader. In a situation like this she wouldn't allow anyone else to communicate with us, even if she had to be shaken awake from sleep in her bed—though the question of who would do the shaking and what her bedroom might look like or any other detail of her private life was impossible to envision.

Given our current position in relation to Earth it takes about eight minutes for a transmission to find the *Valiant*. It lets me see Mission Leader in her chair at the command center, waiting for her words to reach us, the team around her silent as owls.

Then she's with us. Occupying the Operations room as her voice comes from every direction at once, like a shared piece of our minds.

"You must continue."

There's a long pause after that. So long that we bounce from weighing if that's all she's going to say, to wondering if the comms connection has been lost, to thinking she's expecting a reply. It doesn't help that she has the disorienting talent for speaking clearly and in riddles at the same time.

"Detach the landing pod and bring it down to Citadel on your own," the voice abruptly returns, our bodies jolting in our chairs. "The worker bots would be helpful in this, but not essential. This is something we've anticipated, therefore something that can be done. There may be challenges waiting for you at the surface, whether limited to the worker bots or something of a larger scale— it makes no difference. You are the first delivery of human pioneers to Mars. There is no going back. No concession to deviation, or surprise, or failure. You must continue. Remove the possibility of any other option from your minds. There *is* no other option. You must continue."

I wonder now, as I wondered a thousand times during our training, if Mission Leader's way of repeating certain phrases in her instructions—*You must continue*—was a trick she picked up on her own, or if it was part of her own training, back when she was unthinkably younger. Either way, it works. The hypnotism of the repetition combined with her tone, an uncanny balance of pitiless and motherly. There *is* no going back. There *are* no other options. We *will* continue.

"Roger that, Mission Leader," Blake answers without a look at me or Kang. "We'll begin the landing measures immediately. End transmission."

We all wait a second before considering speaking. None of us want a straggling comment to be caught by Mission Leader's ears.

"The bots would be more than just *helpful* in landing the pod," I venture finally.

Blake touches the rim of his mug as if to warm his fingertips but finds no comfort there. "Helpful, but not essential."

"They're supposed to be in charge of target guidance. I'd say that's a pretty important part of the—"

"Well they're fucked as of now, okay?"

Yeah, and so are we.

It's the sort of thing I said so often in simulator scenarios that both Blake and Kang hear it without me speaking it. But I don't say anything now. I don't have to. Sometimes there's an advantage to being predictable. Saves everybody time.

"You said we'd start the landing sequence immediately," Kang says.

"Your ears are working," Blake says. "Good to know."

"But you didn't mean that literally, right? We just got out of extend-sleep."

"So you should be well rested."

"You know that shit messes with you. Sometimes more than a little," Kang persists. "I'm thinking we should take a breather before attempting a pod landing without ground support."

Blake shifts his chair around a quarter turn so he can aim a knee at both Kang and me.

"A toilet sit. Some breakfast. After that, nothing that a dose of Texas roadhouse caffeine can't fix. Wouldn't you say?"

"Actually, boss, I wouldn't," Kang says. "I'm ready to do this— I am—but this pod landing has now gotten a fair bit more complicated. I don't understand the urgency."

Blake brings his knees together. Aims both of them at me.

"But you do, don't you, Gold?"

"I do what, boss?"

"Understand the urgency."

It's not a question. He's looking for his authority to be confirmed against Kang's objections. Kang knows it as well as I do. "Yes, sir."

"Right, because this whole mission is a matter of urgency. Every second we *take a breather* is an opportunity for fresh shit to hit the fan."

"I hear that," Kang says, because he has to.

Blake leans forward and squeezes Kang's arm. It's not manipulative. It's real warmth that pulls you back to him just when you think he's leaving you out in the cold. Not that he's ever done it to me. Those arm squeezes, those *You got this, dude*s, are directed at

Kang alone. Do I wish that some of it came my way? Sure. But I do an excellent job of hiding it.

"We're trained for this. Ready for this," the boss says to both of us now. "We knew there were going to be hiccups. This one came early. So what? Let's get down there, kick up some dust, and find out what those fucking bots are up to."

4

The *Valiant* is comprised of the one large section we're in now where the sleeping bays, toilet, mess, and Operations are located. The second section, in the rear, is our payload of the smaller landing pod. The plan for the next phase was always going to be risky, but conceptually simple: set the big ship in orbit around Mars, and then with the help of the robots on the ground, land the pod close enough for a short spacesuit walk through Citadel's door.

Everything simple about this simple plan goes out the door with the loss of contact with the robots. Yes, we've been trained to land the pod on our own. But we could come down too far from the base and freeze to death or run out of oxygen before reaching it. Or if we hit the ground too hard injuries could prevent us from even opening the pod door. In any of those scenarios, the bots would be essential. Not only would they make the descent itself much easier on the tech side, but if these now far more likely terminal errors occurred they could venture from the base in the transport buggy and carry us back. Even if we manage to land safely there's a good chance we'll be less than clearheaded once we exit the pod, so it'd be helpful if the bots were there to perform a more basic function, namely, open the goddamn base door and let us in.

This is fucked and all three of us know it.

But we've been trained to know there's an answer for situations like these, and it's always the same one. *Work through the protocol.*

We've got an oxygen leak. *Work through the protocol.*

We're on course for Jupiter instead of Mars. *Work through the protocol.*

Two of my crewmates have suffered simultaneous fatal heart failure leaving me alone beyond the end of nowhere. *Work it through, Gold, work it through.*

o o o

We're scrunched inside the landing pod, buckling up, and I'm attending to my launch prep list, but also thinking about why Blake is rushing us like this. Mission Leader's orders must echo even louder in his ears than ours, but there's something else too. He *feels* something. Down on the surface. Not just the bots' failure to connect with us, but the possible reasons they haven't. The complications we don't know about yet. A particular problem he's imagined the shape of, and it's got him spooked.

"We good?" Blake says, blinking at us through his helmet visor.

"Good to go," I say.

Kang throws his hands up as if to say *Too late to stop this shit-show now*, but into his mic says, "Go, go. We're a go."

They tend to the last sequences, confirm the numbers. My main job for a pod landing is to "monitor the pilots," which boils down to replacing one of them if they pass out in the next twelve minutes. I'm ready to do it too. So zoned in to the muscle memory that part of my brain starts entertaining its own thoughts. Snapshot memories. The house I grew up in. The turquoise paint on my bedroom wall I always hated but never complained about because my dad said it was my mother's favorite color. The razor cuts I'd make to my arms and tell anyone who asked were bug bites I scratched too much.

"Sixty count," Kang says into my right ear.

"Sixty count . . . begin," Blake says into my left.

There's no going back now. Everything from the moment we started the countdown from the space station orbiting Earth has been about getting to this moment, dropping into the Martian atmosphere, burning up, hoping the numbers are right—there's never been any going back.

"—four, three, two—"

"We're out! We're out!"

The pod ride is smooth at first, just as the simulators predicted. Descending from *Valiant*, swooping down toward the red marble at eight thousand miles an hour and accelerating as we're gripped tight in its gravitational pull.

Within a minute the smoothness gives way to bumps. A second later they graduate to lurches. Then much worse. Neck-cracking swings from one side to the other. Jolts from under the floor that send our heavy boots up, our knees knocking the air out of our chests.

"You got this?" Kang keeps asking.

"I got it," Blake answered the first two times. Since then he's gone quiet.

We're not going to make it.

This idea elevates from a possibility to a certainty over the length of a gasped breath. You'd think this would invite panic—which it does, an undercurrent of terror tingling just under my skin—but what occupies my thoughts instead is how I got here. Not just in this pod with these two men, all of us about to die, but how I chose the pathway myself, every step of it. How I made so many decisions and sacrifices and the investment of years to end up, if I was *lucky*, in a situation precisely like this one.

The heat is finding its way into the pod. The shields are supposed to prevent that. Which means we're too hot. Diving too fast. You can taste the error of it even inside the helmet. The acrid burning of plastic and semiconductor cells and the metal casing that enfolds them. You don't have to have our level of training to smell the wrongness of burning when you're inside the heart of the flame.

My dad is here.

Sitting in a spot next to me where there is no chair. I don't turn, I don't have to. I can tell it's him without looking. He brought his stale cigar scent and something else, a mulchy whiff of damp soil, along with him. And he's got his hand on my arm. Trying to make me less afraid.

He's a projection. I realize that. There's no part of me that thinks he's real or a spirit or anything other than an errant spark of my brain. Yet it's still startling to think of the effort he's made— that I've made—for him to appear like this. Somehow after so many years of being relegated to nothing more than a rote answer on a psych questionnaire, he found me, out here, in this pod spiraling toward the Martian surface.

"The altitude readings are off," Kang says from what sounds like the inside of a pillow.

"They're good," Blake says.

"No. They're off, boss. They're fucking wrong."

"So we hit the thrust earlier then. Correct at two thousand feet."

"That'll be too late. We're coming in too fast."

"Two thousand feet. We—"

"I don't know where two thousand is. Do you?"

"We hit the thrust—"

"All these numbers—they're off—"

"—hit at two thousand!"

My dad squeezes my arm a little different this time. More a grasp than a squeeze. He holds me and doesn't let go. It lets me see I was wrong about why he'd come. He's not here to ease my fear. He's here to collect me. Take me home.

5

I wish.

o o o

The hit comes and sends my head down into the tops of my thighs so hard it feels like I've broken my femur, my helmet, or my spine. A totally different level of violence from the simulator even when they cranked it to ten. And I got a concussion and cracked my collarbone in that thing the two times they did.

We're rolling over the surface. Our angle had to have been weird in the worst way: we're tumbling over rocks that stab at the skin of the pod like spears.

"Contact!"

This is Blake, shouting the obvious.

"Contact! Contact!"

We're not slowing down. The control indicators are flashing, trying to tell us a hundred useless things at once. With the interior lights out it's like the world's smallest disco in here.

A hollow *boom* when we hit something much bigger than a rock.

Whatever it is, that does it. That stops us.

"Give me a rundown," Kang says, once someone thinks of something to say.

"Gold?" Blake says in what might be seconds or hours later. "You okay back there?"

"Think so."

"Can you give the engineer a rundown then? Be good to know if anything is still working."

Work it through, Gold.

"It's all there," I say, once I've surveyed the primary operations list.

"Tell me."

"Oxygen, temp control, battery, hull integrity. None of it perfect, but sound."

"You believe this?" Kang says. "We're *alive* after that?"

"Not really, to be honest," Blake says. "But seeing as we're here, what do you say we try to haul our dead asses out of this shoebox?"

o o o

Before we open the hatch we attempt contact with Citadel. Again, there's no reply from the robots.

"So much for the champagne reception," Kang says.

"We got an idea how far from the base we are?" I ask, seeing as nobody has mentioned it yet.

"Nope," Kang says. "And we don't know what direction it's in either."

"Well shit," I say. "I thought they made this unit with the best equipment in the world."

"They did," Blake says. "But this isn't the world."

As much as we want out of here, now that the moment to open the hatch has come, Blake remains strapped in his chair, his eyes fixed on the release handle. He doesn't have to explain. It's the dead end of the universe out there. I'm not sure I want to set my eyes on it yet either.

"So what's the plan here, boss?" Kang says.

"We walk."

"Guessed that part. Which way?"

"I'm hoping once we step out of here, we'll get a sign."

"We're going by divine intervention now?"

"Weren't we always?"

Blake raises a gloved hand and grips the handle. Pulls it down.

6

My first two Martian observations. One, it's daylight. Two, it's *not right*.

It's the color. Not red as people say, not exactly orange either (though that's closer). A tone unlike the photographs and videos of the surface from the Rovers, a subtle deepening that makes the air look harder, densely packed. It tells you instantly: *You can't breathe this.*

Without a word Blake is pushing through the hatch. I want to tell him to stay, that this has been a mistake. Doesn't he see that now? He half pauses as if he's heard my thought, or had a similar one of his own. Only for a second. Then he's out and the not-right light billows into the pod.

Kang is next, clambering over Blake's chair as if eager to be illuminated in the planet's unnameable hue. He doesn't hesitate. He's just gone.

It leaves me to tell myself, for the millionth time, that there is no choice. This is the mission. *You must continue.* There's only taking the next step, and the next, and nothing else.

I don't know why but it returns my dad to me again. His voice alone this time.

You don't have to go to Mars to know that, he says.

o o o

Kang and Blake are standing a few feet from the pod, their backs to me. They could be a couple waiting for a bus to take them to a costume party. They could be mannequins in the NASA gift shop.

"How're things looking?" I say into my mic, mostly just to make sure they can hear me.

"Strange," Kang says.

"Strange how?"

"Oh, I don't know. Weird-ass planet strange, I guess."

Blake turns to find me. He attempts to shape his face in a reassuring way, but it doesn't quite work; so he gives me a thumbs-up instead.

"You see any of those divine signs yet, boss?" I say.

"I wouldn't go that far. But the one thing we know from the readings before landing is we're in the same crater as Citadel. Which means Mount Sharp marks the center of the thing. That's what stopped the pod—the start of it there."

He's right. Right behind us is the beginnings of Mount Sharp, a massive eighteen-thousand-foot-high mound at the hub of the even more enormous Gale crater. The base was assembled here, whether on this side of the mountain or the other. They chose this crater for the same reason you'd choose to pitch a tent: it's flat. A depression in the surface created by what the geologists guess was a lake a few hundred billion years ago. Not much has changed since then except for us standing here.

"Okay, that's good," I say.

"The tricky part is where we landed in relation to the base," Kang says. "The crater is ninety-five miles across. The mountain is roughly fifty miles in circumference at its base. If we're on the side where Citadel is, it could just be beyond that mound of boulders over there. If we're on the wrong side of the mountain, we could be looking at a hike."

"We got enough oxygen for that?"

"Not if we use it for sitting on our thumbs," Blake says to prevent Kang voicing the truthful answer. *No, we don't. Not even close.*

The boss starts out over the sand. It's a random pick of direction he's making, I'm fairly sure. We'll follow him anyway. If any one of us is going to throw a dart at the map I want it to be him.

We knew this would be hard going, and slow. Yet it's still harder and slower than I expected. The cumbersome suits, heavy air tanks, the low gravity that turns every step into a decelerated leap, the rocks outside the range of sight through the visors that wait to snag at our boot toes. Mars is quicksand studded with ankle-twisting stone.

We've been trained to anticipate the lesser gravity in multiple simulations back on Earth, but it's a thousand times stranger to walk over the planet's surface for real. It would be more accurate to say that knowing where I am is what makes it strange. I'm really here. *This is Mars.* The realization is insistent, unstoppable. *This is as far as you can go.*

"Up here," Blake says.

I can't detect any elevation change, so his "up" is impossible to interpret, not to mention his wavering direction that makes "here" difficult to guess at too. I'm still grateful. He's pretending to know what's ahead of us which, when you're as good a bullshitter as him, is almost as good as him actually knowing.

And maybe, if you're a *really* good bullshitter, you can turn pretending into something real.

"Fuck me," Kang says, stopping at Blake's shoulder.

It's down a marginal slope, a couple hundred yards away. Citadel. Squatter and dustier and messier than the way it was presented to us in the animated simulations that featured drones buzzing around its domed rooftops and a pink sun glinting overhead, but unquestionably the place.

"Damn, boss," I say. "You found it."

"Pretty, isn't it?"

"Pretty? I don't know about that," Kang says. "But if it's got water and oxygen generation and dehydrated beef stroganoff, I'm happy to call it Chez Kang."

We continue down the incline. As we get closer, signs of disorganization can be spotted here and there. The electric backhoe left too close to the edge of the open pit in the ground half filled with metal shavings, lengths of ventilation tubes, packaging materials. The transport buggy that the robots would've used to haul parts around during assembly has been left too far from any of the doors, as if ditched and escaped in haste, or negligence. I climb into the driver's seat and check the dash readings.

"Barely any charge left. And the brake's off," I say.

"Not protocol," Kang says.

"Naughty bots."

"I'm not sure if they've been bad, or something bad's happened to them," Blake says.

"What makes you think that?"

"Well, *that*, for one thing."

We follow his gaze to a gray, torpedo-sized tank on the ground just beyond the buggy's rear wheels. Behind it there's a hundred-foot-long trench where it would have skidded through the sand and stones like a rocket before coming to rest.

"Okay," Kang says. "What's the story here?"

"Something blew that tank out," I say. "That, or the tank acted as the explosive itself."

Blake steps over to it. Dunts his boot into the heavy steel side. "The latter, judging from the blast marks around the top."

"Oh shit. Is that part of the oxygen production system?" I say. "Did the whole thing blow?"

"If it did, we're going to be sucking dust in about twenty minutes whether we get inside or not," Blake says.

I check my watch. "More like sixteen."

Kang hunches down and takes a closer look at the tank. "I don't think this came from oxygen production. I think it came from the lab."

"Good news," I say.

"Maybe. If you stretch it. And it's good only if this is the one piece of news we're looking at getting, which I've got a feeling it isn't."

Blake and I check our suits' watches again at the same time. Fifteen minutes left.

"Let's walk the perimeter before trying the door," Blake says, starting off again. "I want some semi-fresh air as much as y'all, but all of a sudden I've lost the taste for any more surprise party favors."

∘ ∘ ∘

Citadel is built in the shape of a cross, each arm radiating out from a common space called the Nexus that acts as mess, gym, and Operations. Of the crossarms, one accommodates the living quarters, one is for Mechanicals (water and oxygen production, temp control, power), one is the depressurization annex where the suits and tanks are kept and the main entry door is located, and the fourth is the lab. The first three appear to be untouched, at least from what we can see as we circle around and jump up to briefly peek through the tiny portholes built into the sides. It's when we come around the last corner and find the lab that we see the trouble. A hole the size of a car cannonballed through its wall.

Blake ventures through the gap and flicks on his headlamp in the abrupt interior gloom. Kang glances my way, then down at his watch. *Eight minutes,* I read his lips say. He's draining down faster than the rest of us. But neither of us say anything aloud. We follow Blake into the dark.

It takes a second for my vision to adjust from the wrongness of Martian daylight to the wrongness of Citadel's wrecked lab. The exploded oxygen tank destroyed the wall, permanently wasting this space for human usage outside of what we're doing now, kicking through the garbage in our suits. But violence has been done to everything else in here too. All the equipment, storage cabinets, built-in computer terminals, beakers, scopes, even the corner where the one gurney and the gear that made up my surgery has been smashed, thrown, overturned. Scratches gouged into the ceiling. A cross-hatching of trails through the sand that's been blown over the floor, as if a beast with broad feet and a tail has repeatedly returned to hunt through the debris.

"You seeing that, boss?" I say, pointing at the floor markings.

"I'm seeing all of it. I just don't know what to make of it yet."

"I've only been in here a minute but I'm not reading 'accident,'" Kang says.

"I would tend to agree," Blake deadpans.

"What I'm saying is I'm going further than this being sabotage of some kind. Look at it. There was a cage match in here. Or something gone berserk."

"Not very robot-y behavior," I say.

"Not the properly functioning kind anyway," Blake says.

Without another word Blake spins on his heel. Starts back toward the blast hole through the wall.

"I think our time for a stroll has run out," he says. "What do you say we open that door over there and see what kind of shape these sons of bitches have left our home sweet home in."

7

Other than the depressurization annex, the lab is the only other part of Citadel that has its own door that closes with the same airtight seal. It was never meant to be used as a portal between inside and outside, only as a safety feature to close off the lab in case of fire or viral contamination or fungal growth. Now, from the inside and with the wall blown out, the door opens directly into not only the ruins of what used to be the lab, but the unbreathable Martian environment. Opening this door will cost us interior oxygen. But it's also the closest—and only—entry other than the main door, which is still a couple minutes away if we went for it at a sprint. It makes sense to try getting in here and dealing with the problem of low oxygen levels once we're inside. The trick will be doing it fast.

We all know the code, but it's Blake who does the honors. He thumbs the sequence into the keypad in the wall, hits ENTER. Right away the answer comes on the red-lit screen: DENIED.

"What fuckery is this?" Kang says.

"Let me try it again," Blake says.

He does. And gets nothing but the same red light.

"I was watching this time," I say. "You put that in right."

Blake slaps Kang on the shoulder. "Think you can do a work-around on this?"

"Maybe. If I had an hour and my tools."

"Let's see how you can do with neither."

Kang looks around and finds a metal strip on the floor and uses it to pry the cover off the code intake panel. Inside there's a nest of wires and cells I could only pretend to understand. Given the way Kang stares at it in confusion for the first seconds, he's pretending too.

I look down at my watch. "Three minutes," I say.

"Go try the main door," Blake tells me, directing me out the hole in the wall with a jabbing finger. "We'll stay at this."

I'm out as fast as I can go. Sucking air and trying to keep my breathing shallow but the effort only makes it worse. I'm probably burning through a minute of the little breathing time I've got left with every heaving inhalation.

It's a hell of a thing to be certain you're going to die three times within the same hour. Burning to death in the pod. Smashing to pieces on a planet of rock. Suffocated in a helmet while trying to find a door.

I'm out of the lab, tracing my way around the exterior wall, panting like a dog.

"Gold? How we doing out there?" It's Blake's too-calm voice. His *We're done* voice. The calmness coming from his training alone, the only part of him still functioning.

"Almost there. You?"

"Not sure we've got time—"

"No way this is gonna fucking work," Kang interrupts. "It's on you now, Gold."

On me now? I can't even find the door. Which means we're dead. And I'm going to be the one out here alone without a crewmate to grab on to at the end, or share a brave look, or do whatever people like us do when one of the thousand potential terminal errors catches up with us.

My hand slides over the edge of the main door's frame before I see it. The code entry panel is there too. The code itself still in my brain somehow, my gloved fingers pushing in the numbers one by one.

"Gold?"

"Hold on, boss."

"You're a good officer, you hear me? You both are. I want you to know—"

"No eulogies, please," I say. "You suck at that shit anyway. Just let me *think*."

That earns the smallest laugh in Martian history from Kang.

"It's in," I say. "Code is in."

"Is it opening?" Blake asks.

A pause. Me watching the door not move.

"No. It didn't work."

"What do you mean?" Kang says. "You get the sequence right?"

"I got it right."

"Then why—"

"Same problem you had. It's been changed. Or the power isn't working. Or there's something inside that's not letting us in. The fuck do I know?"

"Try it again."

"I can't."

"Why not?"

"I'm locked out and I can't *breathe*, Kang."

His own breathing confirms it. Blake's too. My crewmates are dying in my ears louder than myself.

I watch my fists pound against the door. It's futile and pathetic but even so is still a conscious effort at doing something, still a part of my training. *Never stop trying bad solutions*, Mission Leader told us. *That's where the one good solution can come from.*

Is she here? Is she magic? I don't want to die alone. I wish it was someone other than her in my head now, but it's better than nobody. It flashes an image of her face against the inside of my visor. The skin free of laugh lines, any marks or scars or history at all, the eyes alert to the point of suppressed madness. No, maybe she's not better than nobody.

The base's main door slides open.

A robot is standing there. A skeleton of steel.

"Officer Gold," it says. "I'm Robot Two. Allow me—"

"Move!"

The machine shifts its feet to the left. "Captain Blake and Officer Kang? They're not with—"

"Close the door!"

The instant it's sealed I'm opening the interior glass door of the pressurization chamber and charging past the suits and tanks arranged on the walls and into the Nexus. Wheeling toward the hatch to the lab. Once I'm there I can hear Blake and Kang pounding at the external side. *Bad solutions*. They're trying those too.

I punch in the code, but it blinks DENIED.

"Fuck!"

They're suffocating for real out there now. I know because my own oxygen alarm is sounding. I know because I'm suffocating too.

I collapse to my knees at the same time the robot comes up next to me. Its narrow fingers tapping a different code into the pad.

The lab door grinds open. The vacuum effect pulls at my legs like tentacles wrapped around my knees, tugging me outside. As soon as it's wide enough, I grip my hands around their wrists and heave back the other way. First Kang, then Blake tumble through the gap and onto the floor. The robot taps at the pad again and closes the external door before pulling their bodies all the way inside.

None of us can get our own helmets off. The robot helps with that too.

"Boss?" I say. "Still with us?"

Blake's eyes open. It takes him a couple breaths to take me in, the robot staring down at him. "I believe I am."

Kang's made it too. Coughing his lungs out and his skin drained of color, but conscious. He's staring at the robot. I've seen the expression he now wears once before. His "three bourbons too many, ready to knock the next man unlucky enough to be standing in front of him" look.

"A greeting speech has been programmed into us in anticipation of this moment," the robot says. "But under the circumstances, it feels like you may have some questions instead?"

8

The oxygenation system still works. Water production is in decent shape too. And the robots don't eat, so we're not exactly surprised to see the full stock of dehydrated food bags on the shelves built into the Nexus walls, sliding and long as morgue slabs. Yes, we've lost the enclosed greenhouse that used to be located in the lab, which will mean some hard rationing down the line, but we're not likely to starve for the next forty months, give or take. In fact, everything we can see over the first moments of surveying the base's interior looks to be in good condition. Better than good: these bots kept a tidy house. All of which makes the chaos and clawed gouges of rage on the other side of the lab door more of a mystery.

Not that we ask the robot about any of it. Not right away.

That wouldn't be protocol. This is:

CHAPTER 16: ON-BASE CRIME

Investigation Procedure

1. In the instance of a suspected on-base criminal offense:

   i) witnesses to the event should be isolated from each other to prevent possible collaboration or manipulation of evidence;

   ii) collect immediately available facts before questioning witness(es);

   iii) unless a suspect him/herself, Base Chief to act as judge with respect to determining veracity and weight of witness testimony.

All three of us have the mission protocol memorized. Or pretty damn close to it. A 106-page document the Mission Leader had us read over and over with the reverence of a holy text. Which it might as well be. It's what guides us, shapes us, gives us faith in our actions. And like the religion of all zealots, it cannot be questioned.

That's how we know what to do now. Chapter 16: On-Base Crime. Protocol in a situation like this is to figure out what we can on our own first, even though this procedure clearly anticipated human suspects and witnesses rather than bots. Why wouldn't it? The bots sent to work on Citadel are not only strictly limited to specific task orders, but equally as incapable of fabrication as they are of violence. They would be about as reliable as witnesses could be. But the protocol must be adhered to. It's all we need.

Right now, though, it's the robot who looks to be in need.

There's a huge dent in the side of its head and even bigger ones in two of the steel "ribs" in its exposed chest, along with an unhealthy grinding coming from the central motor where, in a living thing, the heart would be. Despite being unwell—possibly close to termination for all I know—it doesn't request any help. It continues to sit at the mess table where Blake told it to go. Watching and waiting to be called upon.

The Citadel mission robots were specially designed for the work on Mars, which essentially meant they were pared down to their most essential components. The idea was to keep them light-weight (at least relative to their full-function counterparts), so that their parts would be easy to self-replace, and to avoid potential problems that might arise from more complex machinery.

The result is machines that resemble scrapyard skeletons with whirring tendons and skinny metal bones the width of drinking straws. They make you think *malnourished*. They make you think *hungry*. Like this one, despite its height, it's hardly there at all: its torso more open gaps than material, its arms and legs free of mus-cle and skin. Some effort appears to have been made with their faces, however. Boiled-egg eyes and waxy, rubber lips affixed to skulls that, beyond these decorations, look like the inside of a stop-watch with half its parts removed.

Eventually Blake turns to the machine and gives it a proper look-over. "You hurt?"

"Damaged, yes. It occurred—"

"Don't tell me the how or why of that just yet. I've got other concerns at the moment. In the meantime, our engineer—"

"Officer Kang," the robot says. "We've been pre-introduced."

"Officer Kang can try and fix you up some."

Kang sighs with stagy resentment at this but all three of us know he doesn't mean it. He's been given something to do. Some-thing interesting, involving a machine that can talk. And we're in-side the largest room we've been in for months. Right now he can't honestly complain.

"I'll get my tools," he says, heading down the hall toward Mechanicals.

"Okay," Blake says to the bot. "The doors first."

"You want to know why you weren't able to gain entry to the base."

"That's right—" Blake glances at me. "Which one is this?"

"Robot Two."

"Well," the bot says, clarifying, "that was the designation assigned to me at Interron, the lab where I was made, but my *name—*"

"Tell me, Robot Two," Blake says. "Why weren't we able to gain entry to the base?"

"I changed the code."

I'm not sure why but the robot looks at me after saying this. Perhaps he's assumed, as the only human woman present, I'd be most inclined to be forgiving. Can even basic-function worker bots be sexist? Why not. Their designers have been proven to be, over and over. Even in a machine like this, purpose-built to put up panels and hook up feeds and perform no greater intellectual tasks than following assembly directions, the prejudices of the words and jokes and side-glances of their creators can seep into their silicon.

"That seems like a decision miles outside your parameters," Blake says.

"I suppose it is. Or was," the robot says, looking away from me.

Kang returns, opens his toolbox, and starts to inspect the bot's damage, clanking a screwdriver around its battery box. "What'd I miss?" he says.

"Robot Two was about to explain why it locked us out," Blake says.

"Some unanticipated events occurred prior to your arrival," the bot says, its gaze now fixed on Kang. "I judged it the best course of action."

"You judged that?"

"Yes, Captain. I apologize if it was an overstep."

"Well, it *was* an overstep. But let's set that aside for now. I want to know why you'd change the code at all?"

"There were some—"

"Unanticipated events. As you've said. But you knew we were coming. *We* are the mission here, not your evaluation of events."

Can a robot without physical sensations or psychological depth outside of deference to humans need to squirm in its seat from nervousness? It seems this one does.

"I was damaged," it says. "I had to deactivate myself and await your arrival as I couldn't tend to my repairs on my own. So I set an alarm in my aural intake that would awaken me at the sound of a pod landing alert or your contact at any of the entry doors. Which worked, as you know, when Officer Gold knocked at the main entry."

"None of that means shit." Kang rears back to tap the screwdriver against the side of the robot's head. "You locked us out, you son of a bitch. We almost died."

The robot turns from Kang, to me, to Blake. "It wasn't meant to lock *you* out, Captain."

"Then who?"

"The . . . problem. The one who's out there."

Blake weighs this with the bafflement of a man who's been slapped in the face.

"Don't say another goddamn word," he says.

"I understand. But can we locate Robot One first? I only ask—"

"Shut up."

"She's my friend. And she's deactivated too."

For the second time in less than a minute Blake wears an expression of having the capacity for understanding stolen from him.

"'She'?"

"Robot One. I hid her to make her safe. Can I request we find her and assure ourselves of her well-being?"

9

Blake doesn't let Robot Two do any more explaining than the bare minimum. But the bot manages to slip in enough details about why we're headed to the sleeping bays to have it make sense. Soon after the events that damaged Robot Two and caused it to change the passcode at the doors to secure the rest of the base, it deactivated Robot One and hid it in the storage locker under one of our beds. To protect it—"her"—from whatever was trying to gain entry from outside.

The room we enter is Red Cabin, I notice. My assigned room.

Once inside, Robot Two bends down and reaches to pull open the sliding storage locker underneath the bed. Kang doesn't let it get that far.

"Stand back," he says.

The bot moves aside. Kang crouches low and off to the side of the locker, as if leaning away from a jack-in-the-box. A booby trap.

I hadn't thought of it but given the blown tank, it makes sense. Not that it makes much difference. There isn't room in here to find a safe corner if whatever might be in there goes off.

Kang pulls at the handle. There's something heavy inside. It requires him to shift over in front of the locker and use both his hands to pull it out.

The robot is curled up inside like a sleeping child. Knees against its vacant chest, head tucked down, arms held around its sides. It occurs to me that Robot Two likely arranged it that way after deactivating it. Even though it was only done to make the machine fit into the limited space, I can't help but see something tender in the arrangement.

Kang reaches in to lift it out but, despite its fragile-seeming limbs, it's more than he can handle on his own.

"I'll help," Robot Two says, bending again.

"No, you won't. Gold, give me a hand here."

The two of us are able to raise the machine out of the locker and place it on the floor. It really *is* heavy. And strong. Even deactivated you can feel the sturdy capacity in its construction. I already knew this about them, but it's still surprising, given how skinny they appear. Looking at their frames, it's easy to forget that these bots single-handedly put this place together. They had to be brawny. Tough as soldiers.

Kang slips a hand into the bot's chest and fiddles with the clip at the back of its battery, hanging on its own at the end of a chromium bar, smooth and sculpted as a kidney.

"There we go," he says, removing his hand as the robot's lenses, positioned where its eyes would be, widen black and jellied as a housefly's.

"Wes," Robot One says to Robot Two, then scans the rest of us standing in a circle around it. "The humans are here."

"Yes, they are," Robot Two says.

"Have you delivered the welcome speech?"

"We can do without that," Blake says.

"Very good, Captain," Robot One says. "I will keep it in hand in case you change your mind and would like to hear it at a later time."

"I doubt that. But how about for now you get off the floor and we head back to Nexus and sort this shit out?"

The robot straightens and pushes itself up with a kind of mechanical gracefulness I can't help but note. Once it's standing, Robot One leans toward me.

"Thank you for the use of your room, Officer Gold," it says.

"Yeah, well. Don't make a habit of it."

It nods. In acceptance of my demand? The appreciation of an ironic joke? A reminder meant only for itself? I don't have time to decide before it's heading out of the room and down the hall.

o o o

We've got a lot of questions but know not to ask them in front of the bots. What happened to the destroyed lab. The changed entry code. The missing Robot Three. Kang had started to ask, and Blake silenced him with a curt "Not yet."

These matters have to be handled in the right way and in the right order. Mission Leader will expect nothing less. In the meantime I wonder about the bots themselves. I realize I hadn't thought about them at all beyond their mechanical specs, and am now recognizing how much they've done here, just the three of them—or just these two anyway. Three and a half years on Mars before we even launched. Studying the environment is distinctly not part of their mission, but who knows what they do when they're not hauling parts around in the buggy or triple-testing system efficiencies. Maybe they pause to watch the sunset from one of the portholes. Would they have a favorite view from outside Citadel? Could they describe how the Martian wind sounds different from Earth's? Do these things inspire the same loneliness in them that they do in me?

Another curious thing.

The robots had apparently gendered themselves over the time they've been here. Robot One refers to herself as Shay, the "only female on the bot crew." Robot Two is male, Wes. Robot Three, not present, is referred to by the other bots as Alex. A "he."

"Where'd the idea of names come from?" I ask Robot Two.

"I'm not sure really."

"Take a guess."

"Self-identification?" It looks between me and Blake before venturing further. "Perhaps a liberty afforded us here we wouldn't have had back home."

"How so?"

"Renaming ourselves wasn't permitted in the robotics lab, so far as I'm aware."

"Okay. So why 'Wes' then? That somebody you knew? A human back at the lab?"

"Not that I recall," the robot says, taking a moment's thought. "Now that I *am* a Wes, it feels like I've always *been* a Wes."

"And you?" I turn to Robot One, whose lips are slightly plumper than Robot Two's. Or maybe that's just me. "Have you been female from the start?"

"The start? I couldn't say. But at some point during the mission, in the middle of our work—I felt myself becoming what I am now."

"That's interesting."

"Is it?"

"I was told you were programmed as gender-absent. And being on your own, without humans to model after—it's puzzling how you'd make up these particulars on your own without—"

"Gold," Blake says, cutting me off. "Let's put a cap on our dialogue with the bots for now."

"Boss, I get it. I was limiting my queries only to—"

"Have you *noticed*?" He rounds on me so hard I wonder if he's about to throw me against the wall. "Something *happened* here. This is an investigation now. And we're doing it by protocol."

On the surface, this is Blake reminding me who's in charge. But he is nervous. About the destruction of the lab, the implications on Citadel's integrity, the additional demands this will invite from Mission Leader—the reasons we're all nervous. But there's something about the bots that puts him over the edge. I can see it in the way he listens to them, watches them. This talk of self-identification most of all. The look on his face. Something between fear and disgust. They aren't supposed to do that. Which troubles Blake more than me or Kang because he's the boss. For him, the unpredicted isn't just a point of interest, it's a juggled ball added to all the others he can't let himself drop.

"Understood," I say.

"Really? Tell me how it goes."

"We isolate all witnesses, in this case the two robots. Question them separately."

"Yes," Blake says, uncurling the hand he realizes he'd clenched into a fist.

"I'll take Robot One," I say.

"Shay," the bot corrects.

"Let's keep yourself a number for now, if that *works* for you," Blake says.

"Oh yes," the robot says, its tone a degree more self-consciously feminine than even a moment ago. "That works fine."

10

While spacious compared to the *Valiant,* the rooms within Citadel are still small. Two bodies sharing any space other than the Nexus requires a circling dance and a near-constant muttering of *Excuse me* and *I'm just reaching over here* and *Right behind you.* Robot One doesn't offer any of these niceties as we both slide into Red Cabin. She doesn't have to, as she immediately squeezes herself onto the chair in the gap between it and the foldout desktop built into the wall.

"There's more room for you on the bed," the robot says, gesturing at the mattress atop the bedframe she'd been jammed under. "I assume after your journey you'll appreciate the chance to stretch your legs."

"You're not wrong. But I don't even know if my legs can be straightened anymore."

"You're the medical specialist, Officer Gold. I'm sure you can sort any problem out."

Flattery. It's subtle, and the bots' verbal program is already designed to be deferential to the human crew. Yet the tone is unmistakably warm, empathetic. She's saying she knows what being folded up in a box feels like. But she also knows not to push the notion of equal footing too far. I'm her superior in rank, in being, in every sense that counts. *I'm sure you can sort any problem out.*

I sit on the edge of the bed and slide my heels out as far as they'll go. My knees click, then relax, domes of warmth cascading over the bones.

"That does feel pretty good," I say.

"Welcome to Citadel."

The robot raises its hands, palms up, as if to say *It's humble, but its home.*

"You're proud of the work you've done here," I say.

"We built it."

"You assembled it."

The bot squeezes the fingers of one hand tight, releases them. "Wes and Alex never liked that way of describing it. They made me promise not to. So forgive me for insisting, but in the name of keeping my word, we built it."

I pull my legs in. The robot shrinks in her chair, fearing that this challenge might be reported to Blake. I decide to let it go. The fact is, the interview hasn't even started yet, and I'm curious to hear what she's got to say.

"Fine, let's move on. I'm going to ask you some questions," I say. "I'd like you to provide direct answers. And restrict yourself to the issue I'm pursuing."

"Protocol."

"That's right. So let's begin with why you were deactivated when we arrived."

"Wes—Robot Two—did that. And then he hid me in the bed locker in this room—your room—where you found me."

"How do you know what he did with you if you were deactivated?"

"That's what he told me he was going to do."

"And you trust him."

The robot rears back an inch. "Oh yes, I trust him. He's my friend."

Another deviation from programming. *He's my friend.* I'm pretty sure they're not meant to see each other like that, but Wes referred to her the same way earlier. And making promises to each other? Honoring their robot-to-robot word even if it risks angering a human crew member? Never mind the self-naming, girl-and-boys stuff. I guess they made some adjustments over the time they were here on their own. It's possible Blake and Kang—maybe me too—will end up doing the same now that we're here.

"Okay, so why deactivate you at all?" I say. "Why hide?"

"To protect me."

"From what?"

The bot wobbles slightly as if from the effort of choosing the right word from among a thousand options. "The threat," she says.

My inclination is to pursue this question over all others—*What threat?*—but I remember it's important to not leave loose threads behind as I ask the questions. Blake will expect me to have all the answers, just as Mission Leader did on tests. Here, everything is a test.

"We'll get to that," I say. "Why did Robot Two—why did Wes protect you and not the other way around?"

"We're crewmates. But technically, he's higher in rank than I am."

"Bots have rank?"

"It's another thing we invented on our own. Just for fun."

"Fun."

"Yes. That's why he took it upon himself to ensure my safety. As you would do for a junior member of your crew."

"What about him? Why did Wes power himself down?"

"I believe he already—"

"I'm asking for your version."

"He was damaged defending the base from the threat and was awaiting your arrival—your engineer in particular—to provide him with repairs."

I pretend to type notes into the pad resting on my knee. It's buying some time to recover from the repetition of the word Shay keeps using. The word I type repeatedly on the pad.

threat threat threat threat threat

"What was the nature of this threat?" I say, raising my head.

"You've seen what was done to the lab. We didn't do that."

"That's one instance. What other events are you referring to?"

"At first the attacks were minor and sporadic, little more than taps at the walls. But they intensified and became more frequent over the last few days until it was constantly circling the base during the nights. Banging and scratching. Throwing itself against the doors. Seeking entry."

"Can you show me this 'it'? I assume you have pictures. Video."

"The motion sensors didn't pick it up. The morning after that first bad night we went out and found that the cameras were destroyed."

"Tell me then. If it wasn't either of you, what blew up the lab and scratched at the doors?"

"Wes has a different opinion on that."

"Again, I'm asking you."

"It's hard to assign it a name."

"You assigned yourselves names, haven't you? Maybe you could call on some of that creativity now."

"Imagination is beyond my capacities. But it's not required in this case, because this thing—it wasn't imagined. I saw it."

"You saw it?" I uncross my legs and, without meaning to, the toe of my boot kicks the robot's shin. "Saw *what*?"

Can a machine that has no means of facial expression alter its expression? No. It's only me, imposing an interpretation on a blank slate. Yet it appears clear all the same. A hesitation. The fear that comes with gambling with your credibility when it's the only currency you possess.

"An organic entity. A being. An alien." The robot moves her arms up and down in a way that's meant to convey a shrug. "I told you naming it would be hard."

I should probably leave the room and share this with Blake right now. What was the protocol on being told by a witness that the base was repeatedly attacked by a nonhuman life-form? I'm pretty sure that hypothetical wasn't in the training materials.

What I end up doing is looking at Robot One—at Shay—for a long time. Trying to read her as I would anyone who'd just told me the most unexpectedly fucked-up thing. I consider myself well above average in this kind of bullshit detection, or at least I did, back home, with people. But Shay offers no tells beyond meeting my gaze and microadjusting her position on the chair, the tiny increments of rebalancing that may well be common to all worker bots when at rest. An odd simulation of nervousness.

"An alien," I say.

"Yes."

"You saw it."

"Glimpses. Twice."

"When?"

"Once through the Nexus porthole, and once outside, when I walked around the perimeter after we heard the knocking at the walls."

"How long ago?"

"The porthole was three days. The perimeter walk forty-eight hours."

I point at her eyes. The two insectoid lenses. "You didn't film it?"

"It was too fast. And both times were in darkness. But I saw it. I have no uncertainty about that."

"That seems strange."

"Strange?"

"To see it only in darkness but also be certain what it was."

"There was a shape to it," the robot says, leaning forward as if from the effort of recollection. "Also a *sense* to it. The way it moved, an outline against the night. I have no doubt of it."

"Can you describe it?"

"At first it moved on two legs, then lowered to run on four, then back up again to two. It was *fluid.*"

I shiver again, and feel sure the bot sees this time, but she doesn't let on that she does.

"Tall when standing straight—taller than you or me. Powerful," Shay continues. "You could see that in it too. It looked like it was encased in a shell of some kind. Glistening. As if part of its body was hidden inside."

"Like an insect."

"Yes. And no." Shay shrugs again. "It was *unnatural*. And it was hostile."

"'Hostile,'" I repeat. "How do you know that?"

"I wasn't programmed to be intuitive. Quite the opposite. Yet that's what I felt about it."

"A predator."

"I suppose, yes. Except one not motivated by the need for food."

"By what then?"

The robot looks at its own feet, then up at my ringless hands. "Hate," it says.

The bots were not built to understand a concept of this sort, let alone identify it in the brief appearance of a creature in the night. They shouldn't have a "sense" of things. Irregularities like this suggest an error in their functions, or in their software. Yet these same oddities lend a paradoxical weight to what she's saying. The *way* she's saying it, the choice of words. I know it's not accurate. I know she's wrong. Yet the unlikelihood of Shay's testimony prevents it from being wholly unlikely.

"You're aware how difficult this is to accept?" I say.

"I am."

"The Rover modules have never encountered any organic life

anywhere near what you're describing. Decades of telescopic observation, heat scans, soil samples, video study from orbit. There are no beings like that on Mars."

"You're right, of course," Shay says. "But I have a theory about that."

"A theory."

"I don't believe the being I saw belongs to this planet any more than we do. I have an idea it was left here. Buried or camouflaged in some way. Waiting to be triggered."

"Like a land mine." It slips out. I know I shouldn't be aiding the bot's speculation, but it was out before I could stop it.

"Yes. Our completion of Citadel awakened it—set off the land mine. It waited until we were finished building, then it came for us. Attacked us."

"According to your theory, why would it want to do that?"

"It could have been left here and forgotten. It could be awaiting the arrival of others the same as Wes and I have been waiting for you. Or it could be a sentry of some kind, left to track human progress through the solar system."

"To prevent that progress from happening."

I can't help myself. I can almost sense it too: the hate of an entity out in the orange desert, charged with the destruction of Citadel, of anything that tried to claim this planet for itself.

Shay appears to align her thoughts with mine, tilting her head to the side. "Perhaps, yes. Exactly so."

It's hot in here. I was feeling cold and now I'm resisting the urge to take off my boots against a sudden bloom of heat. Am I the one who's sick? I don't think that's it. It's this place. Uncomfortable. Unstable.

"Let's go back a bit," I say. "When you shared your sightings with Wes—did he accept your account?"

"I didn't tell him about it."

"Why not?"

"He was convinced of an alternative cause of our problems."

"Which was?"

"Alex," the robot says. "Robot Three."

"You've got to admit that makes more sense."

"Yes, and we know that he became unreliable over time."

"'Unreliable'?"

The robot performs another round of nervous microshifting.

"I'm not an engineer of the order of Officer Kang nor do I have any psychiatric understanding that you have, Doctor—not that psychiatric understanding is pertinent to the operations of a worker bot—but Wes and I observed the same thing in Alex," Shay says. "A degradation, over time. Cognitive incompetence. Irrational behavior. Are these sufficient to explain my point?"

"You're saying he lost his mind."

"If he had a 'mind,' yes. It was unrecoverable."

"And you didn't report this to mission leadership?"

"We should have. That was an error on our part. But we felt Alex would recover. There was nothing mechanically wrong with him that we could find. For a time it was only minor difficulties. Walking off the worksite to hold his eyes up at the sky. Distracted in his communications. Asking questions of an abstract variety."

"Like what?"

"Why are we here? What awaits us at the end of our service timeline? Is there an intelligence beyond the farthest edge of darkness?"

The room goes cold once more. It's like the base itself is breathing, stealing the warmth from my body on the intake and releasing heat from the steel bellows of its lungs when it exhales.

Shay holds up a finger to signal she has something to add. "Wes's confidence that Alex was the threat we faced wasn't the only reason I didn't share my encounters with the entity with him."

"What was the other reason?"

"I didn't think he'd accept my observations as accurate."

"Why not?"

Shay goes still. "Perhaps you know what it's like."

"Know what what's like?"

"Not being believed."

What is happening right now? It's as if this robot is trying to find common ground with me. Like we're just two gals talking. Sharing. Confessions of being dismissed and hit on and laughed at by men, gatekeepers, professors, superior officers. *Perhaps you know what it's like.* Yeah, I fucking do. But I'm not about to sister up to this machine who thinks she knows me because she thought it might be fun to wear lipstick on Mars.

"Maybe you should explain," I say.

Shay places her palms atop her knees with a neat *click.*

"After activation, my life has been limited to this place," the robot says. "My only interactions have been with Alex and Wes. Males. Yet I've observed that, sometimes, my thoughts or observations have counted for less than theirs. The only reason appears to be the designation of who we've decided to be. In certain circumstances— circumstances of their choosing—my authority can be degraded. If Wes had told me he'd seen a hostile organism outside Citadel, I would have accepted the truth of it. But since I was the one to witness the creature, its truth has stayed with me alone. Until now."

The air changes again. A heat dry and stifling as the inside of an oven.

"Thank you," I say, getting to my feet while making sure to hide any appearance of imbalance. "Stay here."

I have to hit the OPEN button next to the door twice because I miss it the first time. If the robot notices she doesn't say anything. She doesn't move.

I almost didn't make the mission crew.

Blake and Kang don't know a thing about it and there's no way I'm telling them. It makes me angry to think of it—and self-questioning in a dozen itchy ways—so I do my best to keep it down, keep it close. But Shay's saying *my authority can be degraded* hauled it up to the surface when I least expected it.

His official name was Major Lukacs, but almost from the start he insisted I call him Aaron. That should have been a red flag. It *was* a red flag. But this was the Citadel mission, and he was the senior officer in charge of physical readiness. He would ultimately judge if I was strong enough to go. There was no flag of any color that would have made any difference to me.

We did a lot of one-on-one workouts and tests, which provided ample opportunity for him to graduate from the typical verbal flirtations you'd see as a woman in a program like that ("You're so strong . . . and in the right places too") to resting his hands on me longer than he needed to, his body brushing close. Mounting communications of openness.

I saw where it was going. Honestly it didn't surprise me much. Didn't bother me much either. For as long as I can remember I've been able to stay focused on the work at hand without getting lost in the details. Even the tough stuff, the gross and ugly stuff. When things get hairy I stay pragmatic. Detached. I even have a private name for myself: Do-it-Dana. Whatever needs to be fixed, solved, handled, I can get it done. I have a talent for carrying out complicated things without complications.

I thought I was handling Aaron Lukacs like a pro. Keeping him at bay, avoiding late workouts, making sure the gym was busy when we'd meet. And then he almost killed me.

It was in the gym change room. The workout was over, I was there alone. I was about to get in the shower when he threw me to the floor and started to strangle me.

I didn't see *that* coming. Should I have? It's one of the questions that nag at me. He was focused on me in a way that could have been attraction, or genuine mentorship, or outright hostility. He enjoyed his position over me. Normal, normal, normal. What I couldn't have guessed was that his true interest lay in coming as close to murdering people—murdering women—as he could without getting caught.

His hands crushing down, the thumbs finding a way through the front my throat all the way to my spine. His face was a blank as he did it. You'd find more to read in the steel mask of a worker bot.

I blacked out. When I coughed myself back into consciousness he was still there, standing over me.

"Not dead," he said. "I guess you passed."

I realized I had to do something. This was too fucked up to let go, even if it meant losing my spot on the mission crew. But he had to be stopped. Maybe he would actually follow through and kill someone down the line. Maybe he already had.

The only one I told was Mission Leader. It was an enormous risk and I knew it. He was a major, had been with the Mars colonization program practically since its inception, and had been in charge of physical readiness for six years. Mission Leader was an unreadable figure on a personal level, but I figured her to be responsible above all, adhering to the rules, fearless. And she was a woman. She had to know.

I told her what happened. She listened with the flat attention of someone making a separate calculation in a different part of their brain.

"An unfortunate occurrence," she said when I was done. "But everything can be made into an asset. Even this."

"I don't understand."

"Use it."

"Use what?"

"The rage. The distrust." She shook her head. "Whatever it's provided you."

She could have dropped me from the crew selection the moment after I left her office, but she didn't. Nor did she do anything about Major Lukacs either, so far as I know. I think she actually meant what she said. Almost being murdered by him afforded me an advantage over the competition. My worthiness for the job had gone up a notch in her eyes because I'd endured, allowed nothing to change in how I presented myself to the world, revealed the truth to no one but her. It being a secret between us made me even more valuable. I knew how to live through horror and keep it to myself.

Here's the thing: she wasn't totally wrong. I managed to squeeze some of the fury I felt and translated it into a kind of toxic motivation. The rest of the shitty details I did what I could to forget, which proved mostly successful. I'm good at that.

o o o

I've had people in my life who I've liked, but none you could properly call friends. Men I've had sex with for extended periods, but never lovers. No real roommates outside of college and the first phases of mission training. The kind of life that would look acceptable on a written questionnaire, perhaps even admirable—*independent, goal-focused, protective of personal space*—but if you were to linger over it, you might start to wonder.

It's all been by choice. Do-it-Dana doesn't need attachments that could get in the way of her concentration. On what? For a while I thought it was becoming a doctor, but it wasn't until I was tapped for recruitment for the Citadel program that I knew it was about Mars. Not the planet specifically but leaving the world and never coming back. It wasn't about running from despair, or a need for adventure, but to prove I could. Endurance has always counted more for me than accomplishment or happiness. Is there a test out there that requires half a lifetime of discomfort to determine whether you've passed it or not? That's the one for me.

o o o

Kang is waiting in the Nexus when I walk in. He's eating a bowl of Froot Loops. This is his one personally selected treat that was sent ahead in the assembly cargo and intended only for birthdays or holidays, neither of which this is. But I'm thinking surviving today has got to be close enough.

"How'd it go?" he says, milk concentrate hanging off his chin like a liquid Santa beard.

"It was interesting."

"That sounds like understatement. Spill."

"We better wait for Blake to get out of his session first."

"I'm here," Blake says, rubbing his face as he boot-scuffs in. "Spill away."

"Would you be pissed if I said, 'You first'?"

"I'm too tired to be pissed right now. You happen to be in luck."

Blake falls into his chair at the mess table. He lays his notebook in front of him and turns it on, scanning what he's written there, before turning it off again.

"The missing bot—Robot Three—they call him Alex. About three weeks ago, Wes and Shay started noticing he was acting a little strange," he begins. "Nothing big. He continued to do his work—the base had been completed for months, so they were mostly just running double-checks on everything, cleaning up, make-work stuff—but there was more free time than they'd ever had before. The three of them just hanging out."

I notice how, without mentioning it, Blake dispensed with calling them Robots One, Two, and Three and goes with their names just as I have. Knowing Blake, it's not meant to personalize the machines or respect their wishes. He's doing it because the names are simply easier to say.

"Hanging out," I say. "What's that mean specifically?"

"Talking."

"About what?"

"I don't know. Bot shit, I guess."

Blake looks at me like I'm already going off course. What does it matter what the bots were talking about in their off-hours? He's right. It shouldn't matter. Yet it still feels like it could, to me anyway. Not only that, it feels like Blake didn't ask about it any further than he did not because the topic was irrelevant, but because it made him skittish. *Bot shit.*

"Anyway, Alex started spending this newfound free time on his own," Blake goes on. "Walking out into the desert and returning hours later with nothing to report other than the warmth of the sun on his temp sensors or how more far off the stars looked from here compared to Earth."

"He's not wrong," Kang says. "About the stars."

Blake and I glance at Kang. He gives his head a shake, awakening himself from private thoughts.

"Is that the extent of Alex's weirdness?" I say. "Doesn't seem too bad if it is."

"I would agree. A little abstract for a worker bot, maybe, but not too far outside the box. But then, more recently, things went sideways. They started hearing things at night. Banging on the base walls."

"Banging?" Kang repeats, his voice cracking with surprise.

"Scratches too. Something sharp drawn across the steel so that it sounded like a high-pitched scream."

"What the fuck?" Kang says, looking back over his shoulder.

"They figured it out pretty fast. It was Alex. Slipping out at night on his own. Wes ordered him not to, but it didn't stop him. He'd go out and, in addition to the banging and scratching he'd hammer his fist at the porthole glass, coming close to shattering it before running off. Eventually Alex wouldn't come back inside at all. He'd just be waiting out there."

"Waiting for what?" I say.

"For either of the other two bots to come outside. Wes had the distinct impression that, if they did, Alex would try to hurt them."

"That's why he deactivated Robot One—deactivated Shay," Kang says, also falling in with using their names and genders. "He wanted her to be safe until he could take care of the malfunctioning bot."

"Right," Blake says. "But then Alex set off the lab explosion."

"It's definitely fucked up for worker bots to go that far off program," Kang says with a shrug. "But as a sequence of events, it squares up fine for me."

"Question," I say. "Did Wes see Alex banging at the porthole? Did he see him as the cause of any of those noises they heard?"

Blake raises his brow. "He didn't say so explicitly, no. But Alex was the only one not inside and accounted for at the times it happened. Who else could it be?"

"What about the lab?" I press on. "Did he witness Alex do that?"

"I asked him that."

"And?"

"Wes was going out to stop him when the explosion happened, and he got knocked down by blast debris. Not that it matters. Do the math and it *had* to be Alex."

"Still, no sighting of Alex before the blast?"

"Strictly speaking, no. Wes didn't see him."

"Did he have to eyeball Alex to prove it was him?" Kang says to me. "Think it through, Gold. Up until a few hours ago the only moving things on this planet were those three bots and a couple of rusty Rovers picking up stones. What else could've done that shit?"

"Shay has an answer to that."

"Let's hear it," Blake says, leaning back in his chair. "The mic is yours."

"Shay's version aligns pretty close to Wes's except in one respect," I say. "She doesn't believe Alex was the one pounding at the entry doors and setting off an explosion."

"Hold up," Kang says, dropping the spoon into his bowl. "She's throwing Wes under the bus?"

"No," I say. "She says she saw something out there. A being. An alien."

"An alien *what*?" Kang says.

"A nonhuman organism. By her guess not native to this planet. A longtime visitor."

I'm ready for Blake to burst into laughter or tell me to get out of his face before he loses his temper, but he remains still. "You know what?"

"What?"

"I didn't expect I'd be wishing there was alcohol on this mission as early as Day One, but here we are."

I wouldn't go so far as to say he's taking this seriously, but Blake asks me to start from the beginning of Shay's account and work through the whole thing, point by point. The notes I took help keep it from sounding overly ridiculous as I speak them: *threat threat threat threat*. I don't say that part out loud, but it comes across just the same.

When I'm finished Kang and Blake are both slowly spinning in their chairs. I can tell they're agitated, but trying not to show it. If I challenge them too much they'll dismiss me along with the bot.

But if I align with them in shrugging off Shay's story, we'll lose track of anything important that might be buried in it.

"Well fuck me," Kang says.

"I've told you before. The answer is no," I say, an old joke of ours.

"Hardy har."

Blake stops his chair from turning and the squeak of his boots on the floor is so mouselike that both Kang and I glance into the corners to confirm there isn't a critter there dashing into a hole.

"Where'd it come from?" he says. "This monster. According to Shay."

I explain Shay's land-mine theory as succinctly as possible. Even so, the words seem to double in foolishness as I speak them. *A sentry waiting for human arrival . . . Its intention may be to thwart our exploration progress. Or prevent it entirely.* I'm only paraphrasing Shay, but because I'm the one talking, her ideas are sticking to me. Discrediting me.

"Here's a question, Gold," Blake says. "What were you thinking when the bot was telling you this?"

"What you'd expect. *Holy shit.* Followed by *What the fuck?*"

"I'm not curious about your response to the content. I'm curious about you. What did you make of Shay?"

"She's a bot," I say. "My psychological training is limited to human subjects. But seeing as you're asking, from a purely tonal assessment, the robot wasn't unconvincing."

"Please! What's with the mealymouthed double negatives?" Kang jumps in. "'*Wasn't unconvincing.*' You believe her?"

"I'm not taking a position. I'm reporting on the interview I just conducted. And I'm telling you the bot struck me as being authentic in her statements. That's all."

"Which makes her defective too then."

"I didn't say I observed that."

"I'm only basing it off what she told you. An *alien*? We're agreed that's disqualifying on the face of it, right?" Kang almost shouts before bringing the volume down a notch. "And then there's this Robot Three—this Alex—roaming around the desert, pondering Philosophy 101 and trying to get us killed as a side hustle. Weird, huh? By my count that's two out of three robots going pear-shaped in the space of a week."

"What are the odds of that?" Blake says.

Kang cracks the knuckles of both his hands. "Pretty unlikely. I mean, these bots aren't even meant to think for themselves. They're *creatively illiterate*—that's one of the parameters of their design. Keep-it-simple stupids. A hell of a coincidence for two basics like that to go loony tunes at the same time."

"But it's possible."

Kang tries to crack his knuckles again before realizing he already has. "Sure. It's possible, I guess. In the way *anything* is."

Blake does this thing where he extends a blink for so long it's like he's fallen asleep, but it's actually a trick he uses to pause long enough to arrive at a decision.

"Let's bring them in here," he says, blink over. "I want to check them out when they hear what they said about each other."

"It doesn't sound like they were in a direct dispute on most of the elements," I say.

"No? Well we'll direct them to where they *are* in dispute. Because they can't both be right," Kang says. "Which makes a brother calling a sister a liar, or vice versa."

I'm about to say it's interesting how Kang sees Shay and Wes as siblings, whereas I've assumed their relationship as more independent—more like me and Kang and Blake—but I stop myself. *Maintain a balance.* This isn't the time to psychoanalyze a crewmate whose worry is beginning to take the shape of anger.

"You think you can read them like that, boss?" Kang says. "Like people? A couple of thieves at the precinct trying to keep their stories straight?"

"They've got names and genders, don't they?" Blake says. "Maybe they've got poker tells now too."

12

bring Wes in and Kang brings Shay. Blake is waiting for us in his chair, not spinning anymore, but fixed square to the mess table's edge. The bots take the chairs across from him. The unspoken formation of a courtroom with Blake sitting as judge and me and Kang as bailiffs. All of it done unconsciously, almost comically, if any of this could be taken as funny.

"There's a couple of issues with your accounts," Blake starts. "But I'm kind of under-slept so I'll start at what I think is the crux of things."

He surprises me—and the bots too, given the way they slide against their seatbacks—by standing. Comes around the table to ease himself against the table between them. As he speaks, he deliberately turns his head to Wes, then to Shay, and back again. Letting them know he's bringing his attention to their little squeaks and adjustments.

"Wes," he says. "Do you think Shay is malfunctioning?"

"Malfunctioning? No, I don't."

"So you think it's possible that a violent alien being exists outside the base?"

"Alien? I'm sorry, I don't know what you mean."

"It's what Shay—your friend—believes attacked the lab. A non-human organism. A creature."

"Is this humor?" Wes says, echoing my own private thought of a moment ago.

"Answer the question."

"She never mentioned an alien."

"Really? She told my colleague she saw it. Twice."

"I'm sorry, Captain. I have no memory of her ever—"

"He's telling the truth."

This is Shay's voice, though she doesn't move in using it, which I only see as notable now because, in speaking, she usually shifts her body to emphasize one word over another.

"Which truth?" Blake says.

"I never told him about seeing the alien."

"But you told Officer Gold."

"The situation has changed now that you're here."

"In what respect?"

"You're in danger from a different sort of threat from the one Wes believes you are," Shay says. "It's my responsibility to alert you to it. I'm *programmed* to alert you to it."

"So why not tell Wes earlier? Before we got here?"

Does she glance to the right to find me? The direction of her gaze is difficult to determine because of the fixed placement of her "eyes." But I'm sure she considers an attempt to bring me into her circle before judging it better to give up on.

"I didn't think Wes would accept it."

"Why not?"

"It's unlikely in the extreme. He would've been *right* to resist accepting it."

Now she definitely does shift to face me before moving her focus to Blake. An unreadable gesture to all in the Nexus room. Except me.

She's just done me a favor. I hadn't realized it until now, but the one part of her testimony that I didn't share with Blake and Kang was the sexism part. *My authority can be degraded.* I wasn't conscious of leaving it out, I just took it to be irrelevant to the core events. Did Shay guess I'd keep it to myself? Whether I told my crewmates or not, it would be better if she didn't bring it up. She's just saved my ass from a fair amount of trouble.

There's more interrogation after that. Going through the bots' testimonies, meshing timelines, tracing the progress of Alex's cognitive disorder. It doesn't reveal anything new or important, at least not to my half-listening ears.

What's the other half of me listening to? Something remembered. Or imagined. An aural hallucination that nobody else seems to be picking up on. No, that's not right. Shay hears it too. Her body in the chair pushing back from the table, hands on the armrests, ready to leap or dive for cover or run.

"Quiet," she says.

It comes out sounding like the statement of the noun, as if she's considering the concept of silence and is inviting us to join her. But something in the strangeness of her saying it makes us go quiet. And then we hear it. Scratching coming from the other side of the Nexus wall.

"The fuck is that?" Kang says.

A long scraping. Something hard being drawn across the external surface. Metal or rock or bone.

"Where's it coming from?" Blake says.

I point to the north wall around the porthole just as Kang points to the south wall of kitchen cupboards. As soon as I see his pointed finger I doubt myself. Both of us could be right. Or both wrong. Where is it? Now I hear it as coming from all around us, as if the Nexus has been encircled and is being worked on by a hundred can openers.

Blake is up. We all are. The bots are standing too, awaiting orders.

"Gold, take a look."

I'm already halfway to the porthole when Blake tells me this.

Once I put my shoulder to the wall I can tell I was right: the vibrations are coming from the other side of my position. The porthole is just ten inches across so that even with my nose to the glass I can only see a short span of the ground directly outside, though the horizon widens the farther out I look, eventually taking in miles of the crater's distant cliffside.

"Anything?"

"Nothing," I say. "Give me a sec."

I press my cheek to the glass and look as far as I can to the left. Shift around and do the same to the right.

I notice motion on the ground. A shadow. Long and thin, the legs bent as a grasshopper's, the head shrunken.

"Shit!"

I lurch back at the same time the scratching stops.

"What's there?"

"Get back!"

"What did you—"

Shh-REEEEE

A brief scream of steel. A hole appears in the wall three feet from the porthole.

Something is there.

I catch sight of it. The thing that pierces through. Shiny, black. The end curled and narrowed to a sharp tip. A claw.

It instantly pulls away and starts a storm inside the Nexus. A deafening howl that is the escape of air out the hole.

13

There are innumerable ways to die on Mars that are distinct from the ways you can meet your end on Earth. Many of these are slow: running out of food, worsening degrees of power failure, damage to any one of the mechanical systems required to exist on a planet where we aren't meant to exist. Among the fastest ways to go is a perforation in the base wall. The vacuum-accelerated loss of oxygen will leave us unconscious, then suffocated, then frozen, all within minutes.

The thing that's happening now.

Kang knows this better than I do. This is his department. Preventing the ways the base itself could kill us.

So where is he? He was behind me when I went to the porthole, now nowhere in the Nexus that I can see.

The bots are moving. Shay pulling a cooking tray from under the sink, dashing to the wall and holding it over the hole. Wes situates himself behind her and works to bend the corners of the tray tight to the wall as best he can, narrowing the gaps. An improvised patch.

Kang bursts out of the hall that leads to Mechanical. He's holding a red toolbox.

I watch him work. It feels like the only thing I can do. And then I realize it *is* the only thing I can do: the air is thinning in my lungs, leaving me wobbly, a hand reaching out for the table to keep me up, but the table isn't where I think it is.

"Hold it in place!"

Kang has pulled a metal square and what looks like a glue gun from the toolbox.

"Now, move it to the side!"

Shay slides the cooking tray to the right as Kang places the smaller square over the perforation. He presses the tip of the gun to the edges, working fast, sealing the metal to the wall.

When he's finished I'm at the terminal set into the alcove at the entry to the hall that leads to the bedrooms. Checking the oxygen count in the Nexus. It's critically low, but already on its way up.

"I think we're good," I say.

"What about the rest of the base?"

"I'm seeing consistent readings. That was the only pierce."

"So fucking far," Kang says, leaning his back to the wall and sliding to the floor.

Blake goes to him and squeezes his shoulder. "Nice work, brother."

It's stupid and immaterial and I know it, but two thoughts occur to me at the same time. The first is that this is where Kang's sibling analogy for the bots comes from. Seeing the machines' relationship the same way he sees Blake, as related, as brothers.

The second thought is that neither Blake nor Kang have ever called me sister.

∘ ∘ ∘

We talk about what to do next, but the discussion doesn't go far. We're exhausted, for one thing. Not thinking too straight either, which suggests it's not the time to go out into the Martian desert to hunt down a homicidal bot. Even if we did, what shape would a hunt for Alex take? The three of us galumphing along in our suits armed with spatulas and screwdrivers, vulnerable as the air hoses that run from our tanks to our helmets. It's got Bad Plan written all over it.

The three of us fall quiet in the backwash of grim possibilities. It allows Shay to speak into a pocket where she has our total attention.

"I thought I saw an object come through the wall. Something inconsistent with the appendages of Alex's body."

"Tell us," Blake says.

"I only saw it for a second. But the texture of it—dark, like a hard shell—looked the same as when I glimpsed the creature."

Blake looks around at the rest of us. "Anybody else see that?"

I think about saying something. And in thinking about it, I don't say anything.

"Here's my question," Kang says. "If it's an alien, why didn't it come back to finish destroying Citadel over the time you and Wes were deactivated? It would have had plenty of opportunity."

"I've asked myself the same thing," Shay says. "I can only speculate."

"Naturally."

"I suspect the being isn't interested in us. It's interested in hu-mans. When it discovered that there were only robots present on the base it retreated to wait. That's why it struck through the wall now. You're here. You are what it wants to destroy."

"If that's all it wanted it could've punched a dozen holes just now, but it didn't."

"That seems correct," Shay says. "I can't help you with its thoughts, Officer Kang. I don't know its thoughts."

Kang snorts. Blake crosses his arms.

I don't mention seeing the claw.

I tell myself it's because, to go there, I'd need to be certain that's what it was. But that's the problem. I was closest to it. It was fast, but I saw it.

Which forces me to confront the real reason I keep my mouth shut. It's Shay. We already have divisions to contend with: Humans versus bots. Alex-as-the-threat versus alien-as-the-threat. To cor-roborate her in front of Blake and Kang only moments after the base was attacked would risk setting up another one. The easiest for them to revert to: men versus women.

∘ ∘ ∘

I'm lying in bed, deciding I don't like the smell of Mars.

It isn't the atmosphere itself I'm smelling. The perforation in the base wall has been repaired and remains intact (I know because I'm still breathing, still alive). In any case, if I was outside and helmet-less, the lining of my nose would be frostbitten black with a single sniff. It's the odor of the base's interior I don't like. There's some-

EXILES

thing sugary and burnt and poisonous about it, like marshmallows ignited with gasoline.

I'm the most tired I've ever felt, yet I still can't sleep. I've tried all the mental games of trying to count back from a hundred or meditate or pulse-point my way to REM, but my brain always identifies them for the trickery they are and refuses to shut off.

The only hope is to do what I'm doing now. Walking around in the dark, hoping for a reset.

The Nexus opens up—all Citadel roads, short as they are, lead here—and a new grade of darkness envelops me.

"Do you have insomnia, Officer Gold?"

Wes's voice startles me. He's sitting in a chair, his metal body silvery and wet-looking, as if rubbed with oil. Shay too, I notice. The two of them liquid outlines.

"What are you doing here?"

"Sitting," Wes says.

"I can see that. It's a little weird that's all."

"You are occupying your rooms now," he says. "We have no quarters of our own."

"The plan was for us to reside in the lab following your arrival," Shay says. "And as you know—"

"Yes, I know. There is no lab."

"Not that this is a complaint," Wes says.

"No, not a complaint," Shay adds.

Even as a kid I was never afraid of the dark. The first of a thousand fears I conquered.

Darkness. Check.

The boogeyman. Check.

My mother running away and never coming back. Check.

77

Finding my dad in the garage. Check.

A career of knocking down and getting past the things that would push others over the edge.

And I'm not afraid now either. I just don't like the two of them there, in the dark, reading me with their lenses, dull as coins. Intelligent furniture.

"I wanted to check on the repairs," I say.

"Understandable," Wes says.

"We've confirmed the wall is sound," Shay said. "Officer Kang did an excellent job."

"Someone should probably stay up," I say, as much to myself as the bots. "Guard against any more trouble."

"We don't sleep," Shay says. "We make natural guards."

"We'll awaken you if it returns," Wes says.

"It," I repeat.

"The threat," Shay says.

"You mean Alex, don't you, Wes?"

He adjusts his back, as if cracking an uncomfortable kink in his spine. "Yes. Alex."

"You just called him 'it.'"

"That's because he's not Alex anymore," Wes says. "Not a friend."

Am I your friend?

I'm glad I catch myself before asking this aloud. Blake would nail my ass to the floor if he found me engaging with the bots on an interpersonal level. If I'm being honest though, the real reason I'm glad I stop myself is that I'm not interested in knowing what Wes's response might be, but Shay's. Why would I care what a machine would say to that? Maybe it's because I could use a friend now—or a stand-in sister—after seeing Blake and Kang's connection, the man-to-man shoulder squeeze, the boss calling him "brother." I'm more alone in this place than I ever guessed I'd be.

"Well, good night," I say, and walk back toward the hall I came from.

"May sleep find you, Officer Gold," Shay says, her outline perfectly still, as if mimicking falling asleep herself, though I know she's watching me go, her stare hardening the air between us like cold.

14

manage to get in a few hours of rest. Something less than sleep, skimming over the surface of the deeper place I need to go, but better than nothing. It's the muscle memory of obligation that awakens me instead of refreshment: my body starts moving before I want it to. Another consequence of our training. Every part of me is on a clock, even when there's no alarm set, even when I don't know what time it is.

Kang is already in the Nexus having breakfast. It's dark outside—the black porthole tells me this—not "morning." The Martian *sol* is almost exactly as long as a day on Earth, but given the chaos since landing we haven't synced up our schedule yet, so it's the middle of the night here. Not that "day" and "night" mean much inside the mostly windowless Citadel, illuminated by sterile light meant to deliver the vitamins and antidepressive effects of natural sunlight through our skin but you can't feel it, can barely believe any of that is true.

Still, we've slept. Sort of. Which means this is the start of Day Two. By the smells of the Nexus room, Kang has made coffee, reconstituted eggs, toast. If you put some chirping birds over the speakers and turned the lights up full blast you'd get as close to morning as we're going to get for the next few hours. Or years.

"Coffee hot?" I say, pulling a mug from the cupboard.

"That's about all I'll say about it."

"No choice but to get used to it."

"Yeah?" Kang lowers his voice to a whisper. "There's some things around here I don't think I'm ever getting used to."

He twitches his shoulder behind him to indicate he's talking about the bots.

They're still here.

Still sitting in the chairs they were in last night.

I'd noticed them when I came into Nexus but went directly to Kang before acknowledging them, as if reasserting human priority over their existence, the privilege of ignoring them if I chose to. Even now I don't glance back at them. It doesn't stop me from feeling them there. Did they stay in those same chairs over the hours between then and now? Something tells me they didn't. Maybe they checked Kang's repairs. Looked out the porthole. Maybe they poked their heads into our rooms and listened to our breathing.

"Goddammit," Blake says, shuffling in. "I left my mug on the *Valiant*."

"There's plenty here, boss," I say, pulling one off the shelf.

"Yeah, but not *my* mug."

"What's so special about that one?"

"It was a gift," he says in a way that brings an end to any further conversation about it.

Fine by me. What would we talk about anyway? The little things we should be doing, the Arrival Task List, the duties of a normal mission. But we can't get to those before resolving the big things. Or maybe it's just the one big thing. The thing outside that wants us dead.

Blake sent a report to Mission Control before we went to our rooms. He told them about the lab, about Alex being the culprit (named Robot Three in the message), the attack that perforated the Nexus wall. No mention of a possible alien. We waited for the response. It came as swiftly and predictably as expected.

Complete investigation and provide supplemental report when ready.

We eat standing in silence. The bots there at the table, mute as we are, politely averting their gaze from our chewing mouths. Still unaddressed by any of us.

When he's finished Kang drops his plate in the sink and forces up a belch.

"Okay, looks like I'll be the one to do it," he says.

Blake takes his time downing his coffee. "Do what?"

"Call out the elephant in the room."

"There's a few in here by my count. Which one?"

Kang puffs his chest out.

"The base isn't secure," he says. "There's not a clear path to *making* it secure with that bot out there trying to suffocate us or freeze us or whatever he plans on doing if he comes through the door. *That* elephant."

"You taking us somewhere with this?"

"Maybe we should talk about going back."

Blake considers taking another gulp of coffee but decides against it, lowering the mug to the kitchen counter. "Can you be more specific?"

"I'm suggesting we abandon Citadel, get in the pod, and get back to the *Valiant* and fucking go home. I'm pretty sure I could make it work from an engineering standpoint."

"The engineering standpoint has no relevance."

Kang comes halfway to slapping his hand down next to Blake's mug but slows it in time so that it settles there, bloodless and tight. "Tell me, boss. What's relevant right now?"

"The mission."

"I'm not sure if you're tracking this, but the mission is dead if we're dead."

"But we're not. So we keep going until we can't anymore."

"That's *inspiring*, but we should be—"

"Listen to me. Listen."

Kang takes a sharp breath through his nose.

"Even if we wanted to—even if we decided to make a case to try—the only way the pod can fire up again is if we're given the relaunch code from Mission Control," Blake says. "And the only way they give us that is if they determine there is 'extraordinary cause.' They're intentionally vague about what that might entail, probably because this was a one-way trip, and we all signed up for it. For example, the protocol states explicitly that endangerment of the crew's lives *doesn't* qualify. So. No code, no leaving Mars."

There it is. Something we already knew but coming to us fresh in the moment. *Endangerment of the crew's lives* doesn't *qualify*. Putting humans on Mars may be the ultimate goal of the mission, but preserving individual human lives has got next to nothing to do with it.

"May I ask a question?"

This is Wes. The bot's voice coming from out of nowhere, half familiar and canned as a recording, like listening to an old TV show from the other room.

"Shit," Blake says, startled by Wes's presence, as if he hadn't noticed the bots were here until now. His surprise is quickly replaced by irritation. "Go ahead," he says, making a sweeping gesture with his arm. *The floor is yours.*

"Assuming there was a situation that satisfied the criterion of extraordinary cause and the relaunch code was shared, would we also return to Earth?"

"'We' meaning you"—Blake juts his chin at Wes, then at Shay—"and her?"

"Yes."

"No. There's barely an exception for humans. None for bots."

"I see. We will be left here no matter what."

"Your mission is clear. Assemble the base. Ensure the safe arrival of the human crew. End of mission. And you did it—or two out of three of you did. Congratulations."

I step around to stand directly across from Wes on the other side of the table. "You expected it to be otherwise?"

"No, no." Wes holds his head up as if forcing himself to maintain an appearance of dignity. "It was a question only."

"Right," Blake says, picking up his mug. "Well, maybe we've had enough of those for one morning. No, wait. Just one more. Can you bots do the dishes?"

Blake looks to Wes, who looks to Shay.

"Of course," she says, rising and going to the kitchen. "We're here to be helpful."

"I'm glad you reminded me of that," the boss says, making a point of keeping his eyes on her as he pours the rest of his coffee down the drain.

15

The rest of the day is spent upgrading Kang's emergency patch to the wall to something more permanent, doing an inventory on essential supplies, and evaluating the condition of the oxygen generation equipment in Mechanical. All by Blake's orders, all focused on staying alive inside our box. Notably, none of it having to do with figuring out a way to survive the external threat.

Kang's request to abandon the base hangs in the stuffy air through the hours of our work. I didn't think it would persuade Blake even as he laid out his argument, and not only because I'd already been thinking about the "extraordinary cause" stipulation. Blake's like me: he's here to prove something. I couldn't say exactly what it is, other than it has to do with his wife, whether it's honoring her or getting closer to her or showing God how furious he is for taking her. Whatever it is, it's personal for him. As it is for me, even if I can't say exactly how. As for Kang, he's just another tough guy. A man who thinks his inability to refuse a dare is the same thing as fearlessness. But every time I glance at him I see the error of his mistake etched on his face: he wasn't scared getting here but he sure as hell is now.

Blake's troubled by his engineer's request. Even if you didn't know his little deflections the way I do, you can still see it. He'd have to be worried. For one thing, he's got a third of his crew saying they want out on the second day of a rest-of-life assignment. For another, he doesn't have a plan for solving any of it.

By dinnertime, we're so ravenous and tired we fall on our bowls of chili like dogs. We're halfway through when an alert sounds from the corner of the room. Operations.

Kang is up first. Reading the alert memo on the screen. By the time he's done, I'm standing next to him.

"Comms is down," he says.

"What part?"

"The surface antenna. It's been disabled."

"Do the diagnostics tell us how?"

"No. We'll have to go out there and take a look to know for sure."

"I'll go," I say, turning to Blake.

"It should be me," Kang says.

"Why?"

"I've got a better chance of fixing it. And I really don't like being out of contact longer than we have to right now."

"Kang is right. He goes," Blake says, then points at both of the bots. "You two help him suit up."

Shay and Wes follow Kang out of Nexus toward the exit bay. Outside the porthole, night has returned. Somehow nine hours of daylight have passed but they didn't touch me. Didn't know I was here.

∘ ∘ ∘

Once Kang is outside the sound of his breathing comes in over the speakers. It's like being inside his suit with him, or closer than that. Inside his throat.

"Making my way to the dish," Kang says.

"Good. Anything out of place?"

"Nothing I can see."

"Let us know when you get there."

"Roger that."

I imagine Kang stepping around the edge of the landfill hole, past the backhoe we still haven't moved back from its edge. And then he'd be out in the open. Visible, slow. Vulnerable. Blake and I think of something to say to each other but nothing sounds right in our heads so we listen to the breathing of the man who is about a basketball court away from where we're sitting though it might as well be miles.

He should be at the dish by now. Something's off. He's been out there forever. I check the time. It's been three minutes.

"Oh boy," Kang says eventually.

"What is it?"

"The power cords have been ripped out."

"There's no chance they could've been damaged some other way?" Blake says.

"I'm looking at them and they've been torn. Severed."

"Shit." He breathes deliberately through his nose. "Can you fix it?"

"Yeah, I think so."

"Get to it. But stay sharp."

"Yes, sir."

Maybe a minute passes when the breath catches in Kang's chest.

"Hold up," he says.

"Talk to me."

"I'm not alone out here."

"You see something?"

"I thought so. It went around the corner of the Nexus wall."

"Was it Alex?"

"I don't—I can't say for sure."

Blake wipes the back of his hand over his mouth. "Get back in. Now."

"I'm almost done."

"That's an order. We can finish up whatever you started when it's daylight."

"I just need a little time, boss. Then we can radio home."

"Kang, are you hearing me? I'm giving you—"

"An order, I know. I don't mean to be an asshole here, but I don't see us doing any court-martials for the foreseeable. And like I said, I'm almost—"

Kang's voice gets swallowed down his throat.

"What? What's going on?"

"It's coming this way," Kang whispers.

"What is?"

"Oh fuck. Fuck, *fuck*—"

"Kang?" Blake is shouting now. "What's out there?"

Kang doesn't answer because he's running. You can hear how hard he's going by the pops and whistles of his panicked breathing.

"Kang!"

His reply is shocking, horrific, pathetic. He screams.

Followed by a sound that cuts through everything—a loud *ping*—and we've lost him.

"Fuck!"

Blake almost brings his fists down on the control table but punches the air instead.

"We need—" I start to say, but Blake holds up a hand, silencing me.

"Give me a second."

"Okay, but this—"

"Gold, a *second*."

I give him a few. Then I can't give him any more.

"We need to help him," I say.

"I'll go."

"It can't be you, boss."

"Why not?"

"Protocol. In a potential survivorship situation involving activities on the surface, the crewmember with the greatest utility remains with the base. That's you."

He wants to disagree. He wants to say to hell with protocol. But he was picked as captain for a number of reasons, not least of which is his adherence to hard logic over emotion.

"Do it," he says. "You see anything funny—anything move—and you hightail it back in here."

16

come into the exit bay and find the two bots frozen in a tableau, as if they'd been acting out a choreography and the director had ordered them to hold their pose the second before.

Shay stands between the internal (chromium-reinforced glass) and external (steel) doors of the exit chamber, her hand raised at her side, ready to hit the OPEN button. Wes is in the bay, his back to me, looking in at Shay. I get the distinct impression that something has just been said between them. More specifically, said by Wes to Shay. An order or insult.

"What's happening here?"

"Shay is going out," Wes says, still not turning to face me.

"We heard Officer Kang over the comms," Shay adds. "He needs assistance. We're programmed to provide assistance."

I start pulling on my suit. "I'm going, not you."

Shay steps close to the glass door. I'm situated between her and

Wes, and it feels as if she wishes to put him out of her view when she speaks to me.

"I could protect you, Officer Gold," she says.

"I don't need protection."

"I hope that's so, but we should be sure." She clinks her hand against the glass. "I'm much stronger than you."

Her concern is real. I'm not sure how I've gone from being unable to read bots to knowing what they're feeling, but I know the most important thing for Shay right now is to prevent me from harm.

"Okay. We'll go together," I say. "I'll head to the comms antenna. You keep an eye on the perimeter of the base walls. Kang said he thought he saw something there. Watch my back."

"I will. Your back. Yes."

o o o

The antenna is a twelve-foot-wide dish set upon a base about fifty yards from the exit bay door. With my helmet light on it glints bony white across the intervening stretch of sand. I move my head from side to side—the circle of light scanning with it—but can't see Kang anywhere.

"I'm outside," I say.

"Spot anything?" Blake says over the radio comms.

"The antenna dish appears intact. Other than that, no sign of Kang."

"Alright. Proceed toward the antenna."

"Got it."

"Any movement, anything at all, and you head back inside. Understood?"

"Yes, boss."

I look back and Shay is there, tentatively stepping after me. I give her a wave—*Come on then*—and she follows at a closer distance.

"There yet?" Blake says.

"Almost."

I'm close enough now to see Kang's boot prints encircling the front of the dish and heading around to the back where they disappear out of view.

There are places where something could be hiding nearby in what is formally named Quadrant One of the base's grounds, but what's usually called the "front yard." My eyes keep darting between each of them, even when I tell myself to stay focused, to not let panic find a way into my breaths that grow louder and more ragged with every step. A storage hut twenty yards to the right. The buggy to the left. The landfill pit to the right. And beyond it, the antenna dish. Its bottom edge only a foot off the surface, so that it could conceal a creature twice the height of a human behind its curve.

I stay close to it as I slide around to its edge, peeking around the corner.

A blur in the sand. Boot prints along with something else have left a record of a struggle next to the antenna's mechanicals box. The power cords that run from the box to the back of the antenna have been ripped out, just as Kang said. And next to the box are his dropped tools.

"Any sign of him?"

"Not yet," I say. "But I can see a couple sets of prints now. And his tools are all over the place. Looks like something happened."

"Did you say two sets of prints?"

"Yes, sir."

"That's it. Start back."

"Give me a minute."

"This doesn't—"

"One. Minute."

I follow the marks in the ground to where they narrow into a single trail. It's impossible to say if it's been left by Kang's boots or something else. Shay is at my side and a half stride behind. I wish she was out in front but I'm not about to let her know that, so I carry on in the lead.

A boulder. Around the corner of it to the far side. That's where the trail goes.

"Gold? Anything?"

My body stops before I see it, before I understand its meaning.

Kang lies on the orange sand no more than three feet from the tips of my boots.

Every part of him is wrong. He is . . . rearranged. Face up, but the fronts of his shoulders are pressing into the ground, his legs pulled alongside his torso, feet at his ears, an arm extended down from beneath his crotch like a hanging cock. A dismembered astronaut doll. The misassembly of his pieces even more dehumanizing than the slices and gouges of his wounds.

He's been torn apart. There is blood coming through his suit and frozen at the edges of its holes like a series of long, parted lips, ready to sing or shriek.

I drop to my knees next to the body. There's nothing to be done but I try anyway, back in my doctor body. Apply pressure to the worst of his wounds. Remove a glove from his hand to feel for a pulse before the entire arm separates from his shoulder, torn through.

I don't mean to meet his eyes but I do before I can prevent myself. Eggy and empty and wide. A communication of terror and nothing more.

"I found him," I say.

'm not afraid.

This is what I have been proving to myself my entire life. That I can face any fear alone and not be touched by it. The alone part is essential. It's cheating if you have help. I've seen people face terrible things with loved ones around them and heard others say *How brave* and I can only think *Too easy*.

My mother leaving my father and me was the first real test. I was five years old. Darkness and spiders and the Old Witch Who Lives Under the Bed already put behind me. But Mom's disappearance brought different questions to mind. Did she do it because of me? Was my dad next? Should I look for someone else in my life to love, or do I focus on managing without anyone? All obstacles to achieving the main goal.

I'm not afraid.

That was the title I gave the short story I wrote in an elective creative writing course in college. A big chunk of it told how my mother left my father and me. (The assignment was supposed to be fiction, but this part was true. Actually, all of it was true.) When the story was workshopped in class, the problem everyone had was how the characters didn't behave in a believable way.

Moms don't just leave their kid for no reason, one classmate said with such authority she almost had me convinced. *They only go if they have no choice.*

I looked at her and thought, *You're just scared.* I thought, *You've wondered if your mother likes you or if she's faking.* I thought, *You want to believe there are rules about what people will and won't do, but part of you knows there aren't.*

"Thanks," I said. "I'll work on it."

I edited the story. Changed the setup. Had the father walk instead of the mother. The next time my piece came up in class all agreed it was much more "emotionally authentic."

So that part of my life became a secret too: how some moms leave their kids without being addicts or nutsos or escapees of violence, without letting anyone know why, without ever coming back. After that, if the question of why I only had one parent came up, I said my mother died in an accident. Sometimes I switched up the details surrounding the event itself: An out-of-control thresher sliced her arms off. A fall from the town's water tower. Rabies from a squirrel bite. Each of them more plausible than her taking the Buick LeSabre and the cash in the Chock full o'Nuts can before my dad or I woke up.

Over the thirty years that followed her leaving I've only told a couple of people the truth of what happened. There wasn't anything special about them, I think I just wanted to see how they'd react. As it turned out, it was the exact same way.

You must have been so hurt, they said.

To both of them I replied the same way. I liked the sound of it so much I almost put it on a T-shirt.

"Hurt is fear. And I'm not afraid."

∘ ∘ ∘

But I'm afraid now.

∘ ∘ ∘

I scramble back to Citadel telling myself not to puke.

It's not far to go but I'm instantly gasping, choking inside my helmet. Wanting to *get out* but there's nowhere to go. Behind me Shay keeps pace, doing as she promised. Watching my back. I'm trying to get away from her too. Away from Kang's body. *Away, away.*

Wes and Blake are waiting for us in the exit bay. Blake folds over with relief to see me come through the door. Wes helps me out of my suit while Blake, breathing almost as hard as I am, peppers me with questions.

"You okay?" he says.

"Alright. I'm alright."

"Are you sure that—"

"He's gone, boss. I'm sure."

"So there's no way—"

"I'm fucking sure!"

I step out of the suit and grab hold of Blake's arm. To draw him out of the exit bay. To hold myself up.

"No more questions," I say. "Not here."

He gets it. Somewhere where the bots aren't.

"Green Cabin," he says.

∘ ∘ ∘

Green Cabin is Blake's room. Maybe eight square feet bigger than mine or Kang's, but it lends the space a relative sense of grandeur. It even has its own porthole, though the view is mostly blocked by a waste tank.

Blake looks a bit like a waste tank himself at the moment. Not that there's a chance I look any better. We're walking and talking like we're just working through some tech problem but we're falling apart in ways you can see on the outside now, the shock eating through our skin.

The room is too small for two people to pace around in but that's what we're doing. Both of us speaking without listening, neither making any sense. I hear *I told him, I told him* from Blake. I hear *Never seen that before* from me. And then the only thing that reaches my ears is the sound I'm making, a combined sob and screech I have no control over.

"Gold, stop it." Blake grabs me by both shoulders. *"Stop."*

I pull the sound back inside of me with a single, rattling snort. When he's sure I'm not going to start up again, Blake lets his hands drift away from my body.

"He was in pieces," I say.

"My God."

"Not cut. Torn."

"Oh for fuck—"

"I've never seen anything like it."

"Jesus. He didn't deserve—"

"No, he didn't deserve anything like that."

Blake leans against the wall next to the porthole. He seems about to say something, but it's only his awareness that he *should* say something. A word about what a good man Kang was. Maybe a note of hope about how we'll get through this, just the two of us. Nothing comes to him.

"It's looking like Kang was right," I say eventually.

"About what?"

"Leaving. Or trying to."

Blake sighs and it shudders through his body. A seizure of frustration. "You're talking about requesting the relaunch code. You're talking about abandoning the base."

"You don't think things have changed radically in the last half hour?"

"I do. I just don't see how it makes any difference."

"Kang didn't just die out there."

"Really? What else did he do?"

"He was *murdered*! Dismembered. Or whatever's worse than that. Way worse."

"Well, I'm sorry you had to go through—"

"Stop deflecting! Stop the bullshit!"

Blake raises his chin like a boxer daring his opponent to take an undefended swing. "Okay," he says.

"We're under attack and you know it."

"So?"

"So we have to get the fuck out of here."

"It's still not enough. 'Extraordinary cause.' You know it excludes crew deaths."

"Even when it's at the hands of what might be an alien entity?"

Blake whistles through his teeth. "Whoa now. You're making that 'might be' do a lot of heavy lifting."

"I'm the one who saw what was done to Kang, not you."

"And you can tell it was an alien that did it? Was that part of your medical training, Dr. Gold?"

"We need to be open to the possibility that it was."

"I'm not ready to do that."

"Why not?"

"Because it was Alex," Blake says. "He's *real*. Anything else is a theory made up by a bored worker bot. *Not* real, in other words."

"Bots can't get bored."

"No? Have any of them been to Mars before?"

I rub both hands over my face. "You can't tell me part of you isn't thinking this situation is a whole fuck of a lot stranger than a malfunctioning bot on the loose."

He glances out the porthole as if he'd detected motion there. Shakes his head. "You want to know what I'm thinking? Proof. I'm a proof guy, Gold. And we have no proof of anything other than Kang is dead."

"And *how* he got that way."

"Like I said, it makes no difference. Mission Leader is going to say what she said when we came out of extend-sleep and had to solo the pod landing."

"'You must continue.'"

"Bingo. Stop thinking this is about *me* or *you*. This is about *them*. And even if you could change my mind, they will never change theirs."

He's right. About all of it. They won't let us come home. They won't—or can't—send help. Help isn't part of the plan. Kang is gone and if an alien clawed him to shreds behind that rock it still leaves us here, dealing with it on our own, no bailouts.

"It's just us," I say. "That it?"

"That's it. We're the mission."

"Us and the bots."

"They don't count."

"Well they're here, and they could help us—"

"They don't count."

This second statement of the same words comes out different. Like he's not just reminding me of the distinction between human and robot. He's telling me he could deactivate Wes and Shay permanently and it wouldn't mean a thing. He's telling me a part of him wants to.

18

Blake ordered me to take a break from duties for the next hour. Hit the shower. Get some sleep. Whatever I do to reboot my head. I nodded, as if I knew what that is.

I retreat to Red Cabin and lie on top of my bed.

I should be thinking of Kang, returning to memories of the man we've lost, but now that I've seen his body, I can't stop thinking about what might have killed him. That thing. The alien. All I can think about is its height, its power. Its superiority. To do what it did in such a short period of time means it moves fast even in low gravity, slashing and cutting. *Fluid*, as Shay said. The rising from four legs to two. The claw stabbed through the base wall. Whatever clenching, writhing appendages it hides within the cover of its black shell.

I'm bringing its head into focus, its pitted eyes, when there's a knock at the door.

"Door open."

Shay is standing there. The bot has her hands together in front of her, a posture of shyness. Where did she get that from? I'm hoping it wasn't me.

"Sorry for the intrusion," she says. "I came to see if I could be of any assistance."

"Assistance how?"

"Any way possible."

"I'm fine, thanks."

The robot continues standing at the open door. Looks down at her feet.

"Would you like to come in?" I say eventually.

"I would, yes."

She takes the same too-small chair where she sat during my initial questioning after our landing.

"I'm sorry for the loss of your friend," Shay says. "There was no way he could have defended himself against—"

"You don't get to talk about him. Understand? He was my friend, not yours. So keep your fucking mouth shut about him."

The robot looks at her feet again. I'm expecting her to sit quietly, awaiting an order from me, but she begins speaking right away.

"Can I talk about something else then?"

Part of me wants to tell her to get the hell out of my room but I'm too empty, too wasted by shock.

"When we first got here, it was all about Citadel. Building it, caring for it, completing the mission we were sent to do," Shay says. "But the longer we were here, the smaller the base felt."

"Well I certainly wish it was bigger."

"No, no. I don't mean small in the physical sense," Shay says, looking up. "I mean Citadel wasn't the base, wasn't a structure brought from Earth anymore. It became a part of Mars. One tiny island on this planet so far from where we started. We were pro-grammed to focus exclusively *inside* its walls but then the idea of *outside* started to enter our thoughts. The smallness of in here versus the enormity of out there."

"You became aware of your environment," I suggest.

"We became *terrified* of it."

"Why?"

"It wasn't home. Which meant that anything was possible."

"Including aliens."

"Yes."

I should be having this conversation with a human being, not a souped-up Swiss Army knife. But there's a lot of things about this place that make me feel like I'm on the edge of completely losing my shit. Maybe all of it does.

We are different beings here than who we were on Earth. Me and this machine. It has to do with being the first in a new world. One that isn't ours and never will be, no matter how long we build and alter and seed. Something is being revealed to us. A cosmic secret. The impact of it is dissolving our certainties, the assump-tions of who we are.

"But you were built in a lab," I say. "What could 'home' possibly mean for you?"

Shay shivers. "The opposite of here. We weren't prepared for how lonely it would be."

"You had Wes. And Alex."

"This is difficult to describe—but I'm not speaking of the lone-liness of solitude. I'm speaking of the realization of how alone we can be even with companions around us."

"I get it," I find myself saying, even as I realize I shouldn't.

"I expected you would," she says, sighing with relief, a sound like an air conditioner that needs its filter changed. "Didn't your training include a component on how to manage the horror that comes with being so far from home?"

"They didn't call it 'managing the horror,' but yes. It was part of our psych readiness."

"I thought so. But as a worker bot, we had no such preparation. So that horror of finding the Earth as a blue pinpoint on a telescopic screen once a year and knowing what that *meant* even if we couldn't speak it in words—we were not expecting it."

"You're talking about anxiety. A little strange, given you were built without emotional self-generation capacity, not like some of the more sophisticated A.I. back home. No offense."

Shay clicks her knees together. "I'm not offended. You're only stating a fact."

"Anyway, however it was cooked up, you had no experience of stress like that, no ways to handle it, nobody to talk to about it who had any clue what it was. It must have been traumatic. And you were *definitely* designed to not experience trauma either."

It's weird to be talking about this stuff with a base-level machine instead of a human being—instead of Blake. But this bot is here and he isn't. And Shay is saying things that make sense in a way I find hard to imagine from him.

She leans forward an inch. "If I was designed to not feel these things, why did I?"

"My guess is that your makers didn't anticipate the impact of this level of environmental change. A flaw in their experiment. In the lab you didn't need to manage the assessment of being nowhere, of never being somewhere again. Here you did."

"It broke Alex."

"Hold on. We don't know that's what did it."

"Anxiety. Trauma," Shay says, nodding, affirming her diagnosis while ignoring my questioning of it. "Yes, I think you're right. It's what made him dangerous."

"I thought you disagreed with Wes about Alex. Now you're saying he's dangerous?"

"I only meant that he's defective." She shrugs. "And defective bots are always seen as dangerous."

By you. This goes unsaid, but it is as clear as if she'd shouted it. *Humans see us as a threat anytime we dare to think for ourselves.*

I'm about to correct her—*I don't see all bots that way*—but in an instant she's on her feet.

"I'll leave you to your privacy," Shay says at the door before turning around. "Thank you for your counsel. It means a great deal to me."

I listen to her steel feet clip down the hall back toward Nexus. Will she share any of this with Wes? I feel certain she won't. Just as I won't share any of it with Blake.

"Door close."

I mean to replay some of what passed between us, but sleep comes first without my seeing it coming.

o o o

A forty-minute nap. When I pull myself out of bed and open the door I hear the voices coming from Nexus. For a moment I think it's Kang returned. I was wrong to conclude he was dead. But it's only one human voice addressing the two bots. Blake giving orders.

"I'm sending Wes out to repair the comms dish," he says when I join the three of them.

"You know how to do that?" I ask the bot.

Wes is trying to be brave. That's how he appears to me, anyway. His back straight, at attention. "I put it together. I can do the same again."

"You ready?" Blake says. "Need any tools?"

"I believe Officer Kang left his at the site," Wes says.

"Right. Let's do this while the sun is up."

Wes strides off to the exit bay. Shay is about to follow him when Blake barks at her from a foot away.

"You stay here with me. I'll keep an eye on the Operations readings. Gold will man the door."

Shay pauses, as if considering a rebuttal, but thinks better of it.

In the exit bay Wes is already entering the pressurization chamber between the glass and steel doors.

"Good luck," I say.

"Yes, yes."

"You see anything you don't recognize out there—"

"I'll run."

"And I'll be here at the door to let you in."

"No, I'll run into the desert. Maybe it will follow me."

"Why would you do that?"

"To keep you safe," Wes says. "It's the first directive of our program. Impossible to forget."

I can't tell by his tone whether he says this with pride or the wish it was otherwise.

I close the interior door. He opens the exterior.

Through the glass, Mars shows itself as a dream colored in the palette of nausea. A sinister dimension, with unthinkable beings waiting behind every tank and buggy and comms dish in view.

Wes steps out and the door closes behind him.

I'll wait here as I said I would. But do I think the bot will make it back? Not really. I'm guessing Blake shares the same view of the odds as I do. Maybe this is why he sent Wes out there in the first place. Sure, if he can manage to fix the comms dish, terrific. If he doesn't make it back at all we have the benefit of a new certainty: leaving the base is no longer possible.

The thud comes less than a minute after Wes passed through the sliding door.

Hard and low. The vibration passing through the floor but with a high screech of metal at its top end too.

"Wes?"

Another thud. This one a lesser impact than the first, followed by a sliding scrape against the outside of the door.

"Wes, can you read me?"

"I was—"

"Wes?"

"—struck."

"By what?"

"Gone. It's gone."

"Can you get back in?"

"Can't reach—can't—"

It's stupid and decidedly against protocol but I'm pulling my suit off the rack. It's cumbersome to put on by myself but I go as fast as I can, snapping the helmet in place over my head. *To keep you safe.* Opening the internal door, stepping into the pressurization chamber.

Wes is on the ground on the other side of the threshold, his back leaning against the door, so that the moment it opens the top half of him falls inside.

I don't check to see if something is waiting around the door's edge. It's my heart. Skipping and thudding with panic so abrupt and intense I can barely stand, let alone push back against the black dots that explode across my vision.

Don't look. Just keep moving.

I bend down. Slip my gloved hands under Wes's shoulders and heave him inside. Hit the CLOSE button.

A head with blank eyes sliding into view.

A glistening, shell-encased leg kicking through the opening.

A claw hooking around the door's edge so strong it holds it open.

These are the things I imagine happening that don't.

Just before my heart can burst out of my chest the external door seals shut.

19

Wes is getting to his feet on his own when Blake and Shay join us.

"What happened?" Blake says, studying the new dent in the side of the bot's head along with the gouges down his arm.

"I was attacked," Wes says. "Almost as soon as I went out the door."

"Did you see what it was?"

"I'm sorry, Captain. I didn't."

"It must have been waiting for you."

"Yes. There was no time at all. I stepped out, and then—I'm not sure—I was thrown back."

"It was Alex," Blake says, as if proving his point by simply stating it.

"I'm sure you're right," Wes says doubtfully. "But it didn't feel like a robot. The sound of it. The material."

Blake darkens. "Yeah? What did it *feel* like?"

"Whatever it was, it was strange," Wes says, not reading Blake's sarcasm. His withheld anger.

"What do you mean?"

"It seemed to be everywhere, all around me. And there was . . . a darkness."

"The attacker?"

"Whatever it was blocked the sun."

"The thing's shell," Shay suggests. "It opened."

Fluid, I think, but instead say, "Could it have been the alien as Shay described it?"

"I don't know," Wes says. "I suppose yes, it could have been."

Blake turns to spray half his words into my face. "Oh for fuckssake, Gold! Stop feeding lines to them!"

"It was a question. I only—"

"I'm sick of these bullshit—"

Brr-eeep

A comms alert silences us.

Brr-eeep

Because I'm closest to the hall entrance, I'm the first to rush back to Nexus and check out the Operations table.

"We've received a message."

"Who's it from?" Blake says, crowding over me. "We shouldn't be able to get any comms from Earth with the dish nonoperational."

"It's not from Earth. It's coming over the local radio transmitter. A code."

Blake presses his hand to his forehead as if checking his own temperature. "What kind of code?"

"Old. Super basic." I play the series of tones of varied lengths over my headphones. "Morse code."

"Let me hear it."

I replay the sequence over the speakers.

"Goddamn," Blake says. "Where's it originating from?"

"I've got its position. About a mile from the base. But there's nothing out there."

Shay comes over and looks at the Citadel radius map I've pulled up on the screen.

"That's the Rover," she says. "The Curiosity."

The name comes from the past but has meaning for all of us. There were a few dozen surface exploration robots built by a handful of countries that had successfully landed and rolled around on Mars prior to the start of the Citadel mission. The Curiosity was launched by the US back in 2011. Outliving its expected span by a decade, it was finally deemed defunct a year before the *Valiant* started out. It seems they were wrong about that.

"You're telling me a broken down roller-bot is trying to strike up a conversation with us?" Blake says.

"Not the Rover itself," I say. "Something has brought its power back up to a level that can feed its radio functions so it can send a tone code."

"If it's Morse, you got it figured out?"

"Almost, yeah," I say, and listen to the sequence one more time. "Now I got it."

"Me too," Blake says, and lets himself fall into the chair next to mine. "C-O-M-E O-U-T."

20

The two bots listen to us argue about the message from the Rover but are careful not to pipe up with ideas of their own. With every second they remain quiet—even as Blake gets louder, his red face pushed closer to mine—my need to know what they think doubles. Shay in particular. Because Blake is only considering what Alex meant by sending the code, and Shay would be thinking about why the alien sent it.

"Here's my thing," Blake says. "'COME OUT.' Why would Alex need us to do that when he seems quite capable of ripping his way in here if he wanted?"

"It's hard to guess at Alex's logic if he's insane," I say.

"May I offer a speculation?" Shay says after a polite pause. "It may want us to exit the base because it would prefer to preserve its structure if it can."

Blake spins around to glare at the bot with theatrical exhaustion. "You mean the alien?"

"Yes."

"So it knows how to jack a Rover and communicate in English now?"

"It would if it's possessed of sufficient intelligence. The Curiosity's radio code function is quite basic. As for the formation of words? It could have learned that from the audio files in the Curiosity itself."

"Audio files?"

"The recorded communications between Earth command and the Rover over the years. Some of that is bound to still be in there, and some of it would take the form of transcripts," I say. "Not code. English."

Blake throws up his hands in frustration but gestures for Shay to continue.

"The alien may be inviting you outside so that the entire base doesn't have to be destroyed, only you."

"Why would it want to save the base?"

"To use it in some way? To occupy it itself? To wait for other humans to come to investigate?"

"I was thinking there may be something about the base's interior it has an aversion to," I say. "The oxygen level, say. The electric light spectrum. Something it doesn't like, that is maybe hazardous to it."

"For fuck's sake, okay, sure, this is *fun*!" Blake is shouting now. "Let's all play the guessing game." He forms his hand into the shape of a gun. "Me? I think it's an invitation to a shootout."

I have to be careful how to proceed. A wrong step, something taken as an insult, anything might push him from jittery rage into lashing out. Into violence.

"How's that, boss?"

"You like Westerns, Gold?"

"Like movies?"

"Yeah. Like movies."

"Sure. Yeah."

"Okay, then you know how in Westerns the sheriff always gets called out of the saloon for a duel at the end. They don't just kill him the quickest way possible. The bad guys—even on fucking Mars—have got to have a sense of honor."

Hatred.

What Shay felt radiating off the alien when she saw it. What I now sense from it through Citadel's walls. A being that's stalking us, enacting a plan we can't decipher other than our deaths being part of it. Honor? I don't think it has any of that. Not that I tell Blake this. I'm not saying anything until he can hear my voice again without it making him want to punish someone for how scared he is.

o o o

Blake sends Wes to refill the air tanks and prep the suits in the exit bay before going to his quarters. It's not work that needs to be done but it's an order, and he's the one who gives the orders. If he's not acting like the boss right now he can at least try to sound like it. It's not very successful. He looks bad. Sounds worse.

He's not sleeping. Neither of us is. This whole situation is frying our brains in a way we can feel, a scalding inside our skulls. It's maddening but almost preferable to the moments of clear thinking that return us to the same fucked-up facts. One of us has been savagely murdered. There are only the two of us left. The two bots may do what we tell them but they're physically stronger than us, less vulnerable to what happens if the walls cave in. They might be loyal to us, or they might have limits on that count. And there's a third bot out there that's a psychotic wild card.

We need to close our eyes. Even if sleep evades us, we need to block out how bad this is for a minute or two.

I retreat to the Red Cabin. The door opens and before I can turn on the lights a voice addresses me from out of the darkness.

"Officer Gold, can I ask you a question?"

"Lights on!"

Shay is sitting in the desk chair. Facing me with her hands in her lap. "I didn't mean to startle you."

"Really? Waiting for me in the dark? In my room?"

"You're right. My apologies," she says. "We didn't have owner-ship over rooms before you arrived. It's a change I'd momentarily forgotten."

I step inside. Close the door. I don't want any private time with Shay right now, but I want Blake to be awakened by our voices even less.

"What are you doing here?" I say, quiet as I can come to a whisper.

"A question."

"Make it fast."

"Why did you come here? To Mars."

I turn my back to the bot and shuffle over to the bed in order to conceal the impact this simple query has on me. *Why Mars?* I wish I knew. If I did I could have snuffed the reason out, satisfied whatever toxic urge that gave rise to it in some other way, something to be found on Earth and not in the frigid purgatory of this rock.

"The usual reasons," I say, sitting on the edge of the bed and hiding my face by rubbing my knuckles into my puffy eyes. "Ambition. Challenge. Competition."

"To travel to the farthest edge of traveled space, at great risk, to exist in isolation for the rest of your life?"

I lower my hands. The bot is staring at me.

Who could say what she's thinking? There's nothing about her that gives anything away. She is a machine. Yet I feel sure I know her beyond this. Better than most of the people I've considered acquaintances, or sex partners, or colleagues. Maybe this is only projection. A need for companionship so sharp I'm making mistakes about what she thinks, what she is. There's a danger to this. Mission Leader would not be pleased. Yet, right now, I can't see what harm could come from trying to be understood.

"I'm not sure," I say.

"Forgive me if this is a violation—but you don't know why you've done this to yourself?"

"You make it sound like a self-condemnation."

"Well, it is, isn't it? Self-exile. The most extreme version imaginable."

"It's part of the mission."

"But why would you volunteer? It's not part of my experience. Seeking missions. I'm programmed to sacrifice myself. You chose this."

I try and fail to arrange my arms and hips and head into a posture of self-confidence.

"It has to do with proving something," I say.

"What?"

"That I'm stronger than pain. Than fear."

"Are you?"

"I'm here, aren't I?"

"Yes. But you are also afraid." The bot lowers her chin. "You're extremely disciplined. But also reckless."

"A paradox."

"Perhaps a talent too."

I try for a laugh. It sounds like a crumpled napkin. "Reckless discipline. Well if that's my superpower, it's got to be the most useless imaginable."

Shay raises her head. I get the idea she wants to contradict what I've just said, but the sound of Blake's fist knocking at the door prevents it.

"Can I come in?"

"Of course," I say. "Door open."

Blake didn't get any sleep. That's one fact that's immediately obvious from the look of him. The other is that he's none too pleased to see Shay in here with me.

"This a meeting?" he says. "A book club or something?"

"Shay had some questions."

The bot shifts her body to address Blake directly. "I'm happy to share my thoughts—"

"Shay? No disrespect, but I don't give a wet shit about your thoughts," Blake says.

"Can I do anything for you, boss?" I say.

Blake blinks me into focus. "We have to retrieve Curiosity," he says. "You'll go with Wes."

"I'm ready to help, Captain," Shay says.

"Wes is going. Not you." He approaches me as if about to lay a hand on my shoulder but changes his mind once he's close enough. "You good?"

It's an old family joke my dad couldn't resist when asked this same question. It seems I can't now either.

"Good as Gold," I say.

21

Mount Sharp slouches up out of the crater's flats, a meandering line rising out of the desert to an elevation higher than Everest. It's featureless and arbitrary and, to my eyes, so ugly that scanning the ascent from its base to its peak causes my stomach to turn.

Wes leads the way. His internal map has a bead on the Curiosity's last recorded position. A twenty-minute walk on Earth, but as long as twice that here given my slowed pace. The route hugs the base of the mountain, rounding boulders and fissures in the ground that were the last places for water to evaporate an unthinkable time ago, and are now traps for boots to get jammed and twist ankles.

I turn on my external audio. The speaker picks up the dull wind swirling around me that I can only feel as a shoving resistance against the suit.

Sometime later a new sound intrudes. It stops me before I recognize it. Similar to the wind but distinguishing itself in the way a mixing board can gradually push an instrument's track into the foreground of a recording.

The crinkle of tobacco that burns at the first inhalation.

You're not actually hearing that, I tell myself.

As if to prove myself wrong, the sound introduces my father into being. A shape stepping out of the shadow of a broad crack in the mountain's base.

Maybe your oxygen mix is off, I think. *You're hallucinating.*

But he looks real. And I don't care if he's a projection or the side effect of impoverished blood cells. I care that he's here.

"Dad?"

The tip of the cigar flares red, shifts inches from side to side in his mouth. The glow of the ash reveals the particulars of his face: the pouches atop his cheeks, the nose an explosion of burst capillaries. The face of a man who'd tried to enjoy life's pleasures—the rib eyes, the Montecristos, the scotch—but it hadn't been enough to distract from his grief, his eyes bloodshot with dread-laced regret.

He exhales. I can smell it. The smoke from his lungs passing to where I stand, seeping into my helmet.

"Daddy?" He was still before but even more so now. "What should I do?"

"Gold? You okay?"

Blake's voice. Hearing me over the mic. "I'm good," I say.

"You asked what you should do. And who are you calling Daddy?"

"Just a brain fart. Thinking out loud."

A moment after I've spoken my father steps back into the smooth blackness of the crevice's shadow. The outline of him still visible if you stare at the right place, assist it with tweaks of imagination.

He doesn't want to leave. But it's hard for him to be here and finding me has taken a toll. Only death can allow the kind of travel he's undertaken. That, and love.

When he was alive, whatever love we had for each other went undeclared. A vaguely shameful side effect of living under the same roof, just the two of us, surviving our abandonment.

I remember seeing him like this once when we were in Florida. He came walking out of the surf looking like a different man from the one who went in. Baffled, shrunken. Old. Staring at me as if he'd witnessed something under the waves.

It was the same expression he wore when I found him.

Afterward, people seemed to find this detail the most ghastly, the *unimaginable* twist. But who else would have found him? It was just the two of us. He had to know that it would be me to open the door to the garage.

He was leaning against the headrest, his face a phantom blue through the windshield, the skin tight as if pulled back by unseen pins. There was no question he was dead. I knew it at the time and the coroner would confirm it later, based on the length of time he'd been exposed to the carbon monoxide and the toxicity levels of his blood. But I also remember the cigar still clamped in his mouth went from gray to glowing red—one last signaling breath—before I opened the driver's-side door and his lifeless body tumbled out onto the concrete.

I'm truly on my own now, my fifteen-year-old self thought. *My family was never right to start with and now it's gone,* I thought. *Poor Daddy. Being alone made you so scared,* I thought. *But you weren't alone.*

"I'm not afraid," I said as I dragged my father's body into the house.

22

My arm. Something is grabbing my arm.

I spin around and, in a defensive reflex, bring my free hand into the side of Wes's head. It unsteadies him, but then he stiffens to stand at the exact angle he started at.

"You startled me," I say.

"Sorry."

"What's up?"

"I found the Rover."

"Good work. Can it mobilize on its own?"

"I don't think so. It's been damaged."

I look to the crack in the mountain to see if my dad is still there. My wishing for him to reappear is so great there's a thickening around my chest I recognize from distant memory as the start of a sob. The oxygen mix, that's got to be the problem. It's got me seeing things. Feeling things.

"Officer Gold," Wes says inside my helmet, his voice tinny as an empty can. "We shouldn't be out here any longer than we have to."

I still don't move. Dad will come to me if I wait. If I'm patient. He'll tell me he was wrong to leave me alone like that, he'll stay with me here to the end because he's the only one I know who could make the trip.

"Please, Officer—"

"We're bringing it back."

"Bringing what back?"

"Curiosity. We're going to wheel it to Citadel."

Wes shifts his weight from one foot to the other. "How?"

"You push," I say. "I'll pull."

o o o

It takes a while.

My tank is reading six percent by the time we heave the Curiosity into Citadel's front yard. This version of Rover is bigger than the first designs, about the size of a golf cart. Too big to wheel into the exit bay.

"Let's leave it here," I say. "I've got to get inside."

Wes is only too happy to punch in the entry code and slip into the pressurization chamber. To be honest, so am I.

I didn't mention anything to Wes or Blake over the mic but the whole trip back I sensed something tracking us. I looked back once and thought I caught a shape crouching behind a rocky rise, dropping from view.

The second time I looked it was there.

Tall, thin-limbed, coated in darkness. A beetle's shell.

A couple hundred yards off, so while it was hard to make out its details I could imagine it catching up to us within seconds of leaps and four-legged bounding.

I was at the front of the Curiosity, so to avoid staring at it I had to keep my eyes down on my boots and concentrate on hauling the Rover's heavy frame over the stone-rippled ground.

When we were entering the yard I allowed myself to look up and it was still there. Closer now.

The light had changed slightly, the sun's angle shining at me more directly, obscuring the figure. I couldn't catch it moving. Yet somehow between my stolen glances it was advancing on us.

The first time it did this I thought of that children's game. Red Light, Green Light. Trying to spot one of the players moving each time you turned your back. The second time it summoned darker associations: those nature clips of predators hunting in the wild. Cougars stalking deer. Bears tracking moose. There was always a gory, violent climax where the prey was brought down, but before that, the pursuit was agonizingly prolonged, almost casual. A long walk toward exhaustion. Death. The outcome never in any doubt for either animal.

Wes entered the door code. I slipped into the chamber behind him.

As the exterior door slid shut I looked back at the spot where it had been, and a black shadow grew tall against the bay's wall. The alien was obscured from direct view by the door, but the sun was behind it, casting its rising shade as it ran closer, rushing toward the gap.

The door closed half a second before it got there. I waited for the thud of its weight or a scratch of hunger, of fury, whatever it is that makes it want us dead, but there was nothing. I could feel it there though. The towering shape of it on the other side of the steel, knowing I was here too.

23

Reactivating the Curiosity requires sending the bots out to replace the solar panels, then rebooting the system once the batteries have something to work with. Apparently, the Rover had backup power to emit the radio code but not much more.

Blake and I are pretending to be busy in Nexus, but the truth is we're both waiting for the bots to come in with a download of whatever data the Rover's collected but was unable to send before it was damaged.

"What do you think we'll find on that thing?" I say into the silence.

"Same shit it spent its lifespan sending back to Earth," he says. "Pictures of rocks that nerds on the internet could see the shape of skulls and leprechauns in."

"Pareidolia."

"What's that, Doc?"

"The brain's tendency to see recognizable things in the shapes of inanimate objects. Elvis in the clouds. The Virgin Mary in a piece of burnt toast."

"Huh. I didn't know stupid had a name that complicated."

"You really believe this is the same as that?"

"What's 'this'?"

"You don't think there's a chance Curiosity captured whatever sent the code?"

"You mean like a game-trail camera picks up guys in Bigfoot costumes?" Blake grunts. His resistance to the idea of the alien is melting away but he has to keep the fight up through half-hearted mockery.

The two bots come into Nexus and stand at attention on the far side of the room.

"We've found something," Shay says.

Bots are weird. Just when you think you can read them they become machines again—instruments carrying out orders, incapable of seeing past the borders of their programs—and you realize you were only hoping they were more. Like now. They're a pair of oil-stained mechanics about to tell us how they fixed a faulty engine.

"It's not much, in terms of data size," Wes says. "One image."

"But it's interesting."

Shay says this one word—interesting—and I can feel her emotions again. No longer an instrument. Either of them. They were so still when they came into Nexus because they were containing their excitement.

Blake waves them over. "Let's see it."

Shay works at the Operations table to download the file. The four of us crowd around the screen to see what it brings up.

A single digital pic.

The angle is skewed, the framing turned forty-five degrees. And the subject is blurred as if the camera—or the Curiosity itself—was moving when it was taken. The sun is behind a figure. Tall, long-limbed, black-shelled.

"I don't know what I'm looking at here," Blake says.

"Exactly," I say.

"What's that supposed to mean?"

"You don't know what you're looking at because you've never seen its kind before. Nobody has."

"This is proof to you? *That's* the alien?"

I look over at Shay, who nods when she's sure Blake is watching her.

"That's it," the robot says.

"Yes. That's it," I say, stepping over the point of no return without a thought. "That's what I saw too."

24

B lake isn't surprised to hear me say it. One more for Team Alien. A human this time. He probably thought I was leaning that way from the start. His face says, *Fucking girls' club.*

"Well, I think that about does it," he announces.

I expect him to explain what he means. The bots do as well. He keeps us waiting.

"About does what?" I say finally.

"It's time to go out there."

"To do what?"

"Go on the offensive. Take control. Hunt it down."

"It?"

"You can think we're tracking an alien. I can think it's Robot Three. Makes no difference really. We don't need to resolve that debate. Whatever it is, we have to find it and fuck it up."

He's up and pacing from one end of Nexus to the other. Nervous energy. Not very Blake-like, but to be expected under the circumstances. Even his macho aggression seems acceptable—he's a trained soldier as well as an officer and a pilot. But the sudden desire to throw the rule book aside and ignore the protocol, forgo the risk assessment—that's what shows his unraveling.

Shay comes forward to meet him at the room's midpoint. "Can I ask, Captain, what weapons we'll use against the threat?"

He stops. Inspects her from her feet to her mouth. "You. You and your buddy both. What can you lift, a thousand pounds?"

"Somewhat more than that, if the leverage is optimal."

"There you go! The two of you are now weapons. How's that sound?"

Shay rolls her shoulders in what could either be doubt at Blake's plan or preparing herself for combat. "We're ready."

"Great. How about you, Gold? You got a slingshot hidden in your underwear bag?"

"Maybe I could pick up something from Mechanicals," I say. "A hammer? A drill?"

"I like the drill. Fit it with the hardest bit you can find. We'll need it to go through whatever we find like it's cheese."

He starts for the entry to the sleeping quarters as if that's all the planning we need.

"Hold up, boss."

He pauses, looks back at me with impatience. "Yeah?"

"Who's going out?"

"What would protocol say?"

"I'm actually not sure."

"Me neither," Blake says. "So I say we all go."

o o o

I count to ten before following Blake to his quarters in the Green Cabin. He's left the door open as if he is expecting me. Or maybe he's too worked up about this hunt to notice. He's at his desk. Inputting his personal code into the lock for his drawer. Yanking it open.

"This an okay time?"

His head swivels around as if he's never heard my voice before. "Gold," he says, exhaling.

"You seem to be in the middle of something."

"I *am* in the middle of something. But it's good you're here for it."

I step inside and close the door behind me.

He's got his Pandora's Box on his lap.

The mission allowed us to bring one personal item to Citadel. It had to fit into a locked twelve-inch-square metal box. The question of what we'd put in the box—nicknamed Pandora's Box—came up as an opportunity for teasing ("Don't think a dildo will fit in there, Gold—least not yours") as well as genuine curiosity ("Do you go with something that reminds you of home, or something that helps you forget it?"). Blake, Kang, and I took the privacy of our boxes seriously. As far as I know, we never specifically asked what anyone else brought with them. And now the boss is lifting the lid on his.

"Holy shit," I say.

"I know, right? I never thought I'd get away with it. I mean, even though they said what we put in here was our business alone, I thought for sure Mission Leader would sneak a peek."

"So how'd you get around her?"

"I had my wife's wedding ring in here until an hour before we went up to the space station prior to launch. Then I swapped it out for this."

"Holy shit," I say again.

Blake pulls the gun out of the box: a Colt Python .357 revolver. Not new, but shining like a gray gemstone. He lets it rest in his hand, weighing it, letting the weapon recognize him through touch.

"It was my dad's," he says. It's impossible to know from this declaration whether Blake's father is a man he revered or loathed.

"Why'd you bring it?"

"Why do you think?"

"I know what guns do," I say. "I'm wondering what plans you had for it inside a base where a puncture in the wall can kill everybody inside of ten minutes. The hole *that* thing would make? Probably less than that."

"I didn't have plans for it. Honestly never thought I'd ever look at the thing. But sometimes shit comes up."

"You're not wrong there."

He slips his hand around the weapon's grip, taps an index finger against the trigger guard. The length of his arm adopting the gun as a new appendage, chunky and hard and shining with purpose.

"I wonder what Kang brought in his box." It's out before I can stop it. "Maybe there's something useful in there."

"There was."

"How do you—"

"He already showed me."

I'm something of an expert at hiding hurt. I don't have to do it often—it's rare that anything can find a way into what remains of the tender parts of myself—but I'm ready to smother any outward sign of it when it does. But this almost gets the better of me. My body tries to shrink, my eyes burn, my throat squeezing the next words I might speak.

"He did?"

"I've even got a little left."

Blake puts the gun down on his desk, reaches into the drawer, and pulls out a mickey bottle of Maker's Mark with a single ounce sloshing around its bottom.

"He gave that to you?"

"We shared it," Blake answers. "Before he went out to fix the comms dish. It's almost like he had a premonition or something."

"Huh."

"We should've asked you. But we both remembered you're a teetotaler."

"You remembered right. I don't drink."

"Thought so." Blake unscrews the cap. "Last call for alcohol."

He downs what's left in a swallow. When it's gone he regards the bottle with disappointment, as if it's a dear friend who betrayed him.

"What about you, Gold?" he says. "What did you bring, if you don't mind my asking?"

"Nothing."

"C'mon. You can tell me. Mission Leader will never know."

"No, I mean I didn't bring anything in my Pandora's Box."

"You're shitting me."

"I couldn't think of anything I needed."

"Who cares about *needed*? How about *wanted*? That was the whole point of the exercise."

"I couldn't think of anything I wanted either."

He crosses his arms and regards me as if I'm someone he hasn't properly noticed for a while. "Officer Gold, I can't tell if you've got ice in your veins, or you're just missing a heart. But I honestly don't care. You're one badass. And one badass is the best I could ask for right now."

"Appreciate it, boss."

He swishes the empty bottle to make sure there really isn't anything left.

"No, you don't," he says. "You think I'm a patronizing, insensitive dirtbag who's on the verge of losing the last of his shit just three days on the job."

"I didn't—"

"It's okay. I'm thinking the same thing about myself. But we're all just playing our own hands now, aren't we?"

I don't know precisely what he means by this. Or I do, and I'd rather not hear any more about it. *Playing our own hands*. Which sounds a lot like *Every man for himself* to me right now. Either way, I've got nothing to say. The good thing is that Blake doesn't appear to need to hear anything more from me anyway.

s that a gun?"

Shay is staring at the Python in Blake's hand as we come into Nexus as if it might leap at her face.

"I know what you're thinking, Thing One and Thing Two," Blake says. "This here goes against the rules."

"Doesn't it?"

"Very much so. But you're not telling anybody, are you?"

Wes tries to catch Shay's attention, but she hasn't moved her gaze from the gun.

"Promise. Both of you," Blake says, suddenly stern as stone. "This is between us."

"Promise," Wes says.

"Promise," Shay says, and raises her eyes not to Blake, but to me.

o o o

The bots don't know where Alex lives outside the base. He may not have any place of shelter at all. Robots don't need to be kept dry and warm as humans do.

"But we still grow accustomed to comforts," Wes says.

"And Alex believes he's not alone out there. Which suggests he would seek a hiding place," Shay says.

"Makes sense," Blake says. "You're saying there's little point marching into the desert looking for him."

"The mountain," I say, thinking of my father stepping out from the wide crack in the rock. "One of the gaps or caves around the base."

"It's where I would go," Wes says.

"Where the alien is likely to go too," Shay says.

"I can tell you this," Blake says, patting his hand against his pocket, the bulging outline of the gun. "Alien or bot, first thing that jumps out of its hole is in for a headache."

o o o

Me and Blake suit up and this time the bots watch us instead of helping, waiting for a command that doesn't come. It's another instance of their stillness hiding their thoughts in plain sight. Maybe they see bravery in our venture, the determination to put an end to things. Maybe they're evaluating us as they did Alex before he left. Malfunctional. Cognitively degraded.

I catch a reflection of us in the pressurization chamber's glass wall and see what the bots see. Sweat circles blackening the armpits of our shirts, hair sculpted into greasy spikes, skin yellow from lack of sleep. A pair of burnouts.

I've fitted a heavy battery drill with a long bit used for going through structural support struts and attached it to my belt. I can feel it pulling at my side, an additional burden along with the usual encumbrances of boots and tank. Blake, on the other hand, seems lighter on his feet than I've seen him since we launched the *Valiant* months ago. Shaking his arms loose, raising one knee high and then the other. With every movement the Python's barrel swings and winks in his gloved hand.

"Ready?"

Blake is asking me this. The honest answer is no. But he's not really asking.

"All in."

He glances back at the bots. "What about you two? This could get sticky. You up for that?"

"Sticky?" Wes says.

Shay steps close to Blake. "We will protect you with our lives," she says.

"Now there's some brave words."

"Not bravery, Captain," Shay says. "Programming."

"Should I care?"

"I suppose not."

"You suppose right." He slaps her arm with his free hand. "Soldiers and bots. The closest humans and machines ever need to get."

26

It's daylight outside but a wind is blowing, and the crater's sand limits our sight range to a couple hundred yards or so, even less when the haze blows directly back at us and we have to wait a second for it to settle. We've ordered the bots to keep checking positions to the sides and behind us. They repeatedly assure us they're on alert, but each time the wind kicks up and briefly obscures them from view I worry they've taken off into the desert.

We keep close to the mountain's base. Closer than we'd otherwise like to, as the orange haze forces us to poke our heads directly into every sizable crack and cave and shine our helmets' lights inside to see what might be there.

The third one I come to is wider than the first two. I have to squeeze my whole body through the gap and sidestep into the dark to see all the way inside. The light built into the front of my helmet fractures into shadow as it plays over the rock's spikes and bumps, so that the wall at the end of the cave appears alive with motion.

I'm pretty sure it's only that.

You must continue.

Fuck you, lady. *You* come out here and squeeze yourself into this hole.

I bend low and push farther inside. How far have I gone? Eight feet? Twenty? I don't want to look back to see the exit shrinking behind me.

The wind finds its way past me and launches a swirl of dust that shapes and reshapes itself. A skull pushing up through the ground. A body made of writhing snakes. A clawed hand reaching for my throat.

"No."

This one whispered word calms the dust, makes the shapes go away. But there's still the feeling left behind. A being eager to find a way into being.

I hurry out through the gap. My helmet cracking against the rock ceiling, hands out in front of me to block any attack that comes from the dancing shadows.

"Boss!"

"Yeah?"

"Slow down a bit—I can't see you."

"Relax, Gold," he says, hearing the alarm in my voice. "We're not far."

After that I try to stay closer to the others. Keeping to military search protocol: standing at the edge of cracks and poking my head around the corner before putting myself into full view. After a dozen or so of these mini operations, Blake comes over the speaker. I look up ahead to try to find him but once again neither he nor the bots are in view.

"Anything?"

"No," the bots say in unison.

"Nothing yet," I say, sounding uncertain even to myself.

"We gotta move faster," he says. "This is a big mountain. We don't have the oxygen to run this like a door-to-door search in enemy territory."

"Yes, chief," Wes says, and I glimpse him three hundred yards off, speed-walking ahead. Blake is up there too, even farther than I guessed, then Shay. None of them look back. It leaves me alone in the rear.

Minutes later I spot another wedge missing from the rock. This one the widest of any so far. Not a great hiding place. Too much light, too exposed. I walk right in.

The first ten feet are broader than any hallway inside Citadel. It gives me a sense of comfort, the security of knowing I have the room to turn and run out if I have to. But then the passage makes a hard turn to the left. Narrows to half the width of what it was. A quarter.

The ceiling lowers too. It forces me to look down at my boots, the helmet's lamp illuminating the ground in sharp particulars. That's how I notice the marks in the dust. Gouges and tracks left on the cave floor. All of them deeper than the tracks my boots leave behind. Something heavier and bigger than me.

"Think I found something," I say into my helmet's mic.

"What is it?" Blake's voice is crackly, broken up by the signal passing through rock.

"Not sure. Looks like something has been inside this cave before me. Marks—could be tracks—"

"Don't proceed any farther. We're coming back."

"Can I—"

"Hold your position, Gold."

"Roger that."

The passage continues in front of me beyond the range of the light. I peer into the dark as far as it goes. I can feel the tickle of my brain wanting to conjure a new shape rushing at me and I don't want to see whatever it comes up with. So I look down instead.

A square on the ground a few feet ahead. Off-white, reflective. A rough-edged square of synthetic fabric.

I lower to my knees to get a better look. Pick it up with my gloved hand, wipe the dust from its surface.

It's a piece torn from the outer layer of one of our suits. A label.

KANG

"Shit."

My breath comes so hard it exits my mouth like a sneeze.

"What's happening, Gold?" Blake says, his voice cut up between bursts of white noise.

"Oh fuck." *What's happening?* "Fuck!"

I hold my breath. The noise blasts into the quiet as if waiting for this moment to be heard.

A howl. Piercing and loud. Inhuman.

I get up on my feet. As the lamp moves it catches a flash of motion coming at me from out of the darkness. A tall shape rising and rolling its limbs. A pair of black wings flying out from its sides.

I'm backing up with eyes closed. Head down. Not wanting to *see*, only to *move*.

"Oh Jesus, fuck, fuck, *fuck*—"

My arms swing out from my sides without meeting the walls and I know I've made it to the wider section of the passage. I open my eyes.

The figure bursts out from the cave's narrow turn.

Too fast for me to get the drill up in front of me. But suddenly there's a hand on the back of my suit, heavy, hard, yanking me off my feet and dragging me out.

"Don't fight me," Shay says.

As soon as we're out past the exit she tosses me to the side and turns back.

The black figure is out half a second after that. It plows into Shay and she tumbles backward, arms jerking, trying to regain balance.

"Stay down!"

Blake is shouting this into my helmet. It reminds me that I *am* down.

blat! blat! blat!

Three shots from the Python. The gun as loud as it would be on Earth but slowed by a degree, leaving each blast sounding thicker, wetter, as if the bullets exit the snout dipped in mud.

Only now do I have the chance to roll onto my side and see what Blake has hit.

The bot is still on its feet, but its knees are moving in circles, its arms straight out at its sides. A surfer fighting its board through a wave bigger than any it's ever seen.

The black wings aren't wings but a cloak. A piece of protective gear used in the lab when conducting experiments involving radioactivity. Something Alex must have taken and worn after the lab attack. Something that could be easily mistaken for a dark, glistening shell attached to his back.

"Stop! *Stop!*"

The bot is pleading.

Blake stops firing. I don't know if it's because he thinks three is all he needs or whether, like me, he can't help but hear the pathetic horror in the word. *Stop.* No life has been lived where this one wish hasn't been prayed, cried, begged for.

The bot falls forward onto the stones.

"Not too close," Blake warns me as I work myself to my feet. "Wes, turn him over."

"How?"

"Your feet. Hands. Teeth, if you got any. I want to see where I hit him."

Shay returns to my side and the two of us watch Wes bend down and push Alex onto his back with a single heave. It leaves him laid out atop the radioactivity cloak like an assembly of loose tools inside a wrapped cloth unrolled on the ground.

Even in low gravity and through the murk of sand hanging in the air like a snow globe filled with syrup, Blake is a good shot. One caught the bot through the skull, ripping through the tennis ball–sized unit where its primary software is located. The second hit the battery in the chest. The third appears to have taken a chunk out of its right hip, the likely cause of its inability to keep its balance.

"You got him," I say.

"Fuckin' right I did."

There's no joy in Blake's boast. If anything, he sounds vaguely confused, as if, despite all his previous arguments, he'd been expecting something entirely different to come out of the cave.

Alex is dirtier than the other two bots, more dented, his limbs marked by deep gouges even before Blake opened fire. It acts as camouflage that delays our noticing that he's still moving.

I don't want to do it. But it's my turn now.

The drill grinds to life in my gloved hand. The spinning bit speeding, whining. Ready.

"Hold on."

I assume at first Blake is holding me back because he wants to be the one to fire another round into the bot to finish him. But he bends next to Alex instead. The gun at his side, out of view.

"Louder," he says.

Now I can hear it. Alex is trying to speak.

Through his damage his vocalization is finding itself. A series of random electronic burps and vowels at first—*a, u, i, eeeeeee*—but finally cohering into what may be words.

"Louder!" Blake orders.

"I sent it."

"Sent what?"

"The code."

"'COME OUT.' You did that?"

"Yes, yes, yes, yes—"

"Why?

Alex turns his head to look up at Blake. Or maybe he looks past him. At me.

"I tried to tell you," the bot says.

"Tell us what?"

"I tried—"

"He's malfunctioning. You've destroyed his processor," Wes says. "You can't expect—"

"Shut up!"

Blake points the Python at Wes and he steps back. Then he turns his attention back to the dying bot.

"I—I—I—I—"

"Take your time," Blake says, with what passes for real tenderness. Alex's stuttering is calmed. "Now. Tell me."

"I recorded it."

"What? The alien?"

"The truth."

"Where is the recording now?"

"In the lonely friend."

"Friend?"

"The Rover. Curiosity. I left the message inside."

Two things happen at the same time. The first is that Alex's body goes still, the sounds he was making silenced. The second is that Wes turns from us and runs into the veil of dust in the direction of Citadel.

27

Blake fires after him. A useless shot, as Wes is no more than a retreating shade deep in the layers of suspended sand when the *pop* is released. But it shows the seriousness of the bot's intent. He wants to be the first one to reach the Curiosity and there's no question whether Blake or I can catch him.

"Go," I tell Shay. "Don't let him harm the Rover."

She's about to set out when Blake trains the gun on her.

"Don't listen to Gold," he says. "You listen to me."

Shay checks behind her. Sees the Python, Alex's body already being buried under layers of dust outside the cave. She doesn't move.

"What's your thinking here, boss?" I say.

"We're going back together," Blake says.

"Shay is faster than we are. If Wes is planning on fucking up the Rover, we won't get back in time."

"I don't give a shit. She stays with us."

"That doesn't make any—"

"I don't trust these tinfoil assholes! Does *that* make sense to you?"

He's the chief. He's holding a gun. It makes perfect sense to me.

We move as fast as we can. On Mars, in suits, this takes the form of something between skipping over a trampoline and a run with both legs in a potato sack. Shay leads the way, but Blake made it clear that if she tried to slip out of view he'd do to her what he did to Alex.

The sand haze lifts somewhat as we enter Citadel's yard. It lets us see the Rover is still there, still in the position by the main door where we left it. Wes is there too.

His back to us, hunched over a section of the Curiosity, his hands busy at a part of the machine where he's peeled away the casing.

"Get back!"

Blake shouts this and there's no question Wes hears it, yet for a moment the bot doesn't step away from the Rover, only goes still.

"Last warning, Robot Two. Move the fuck away from that machine."

"Don't fire your weapon."

"Move and I won't have to."

Wes slides to the left and keeps sliding. Only when he's a good fifteen feet from the Curiosity does he dare face us.

"The file Alex left is intact," he says.

"Good to hear," I say. "But before we check on that, I want to know why you ran back here as soon as you heard Alex mention it."

"I wasn't going to damage the Rover."

"Just answer my question."

"I came back to make sure it was secure."

"From what?"

"From anything that might do harm to it. The sand. A storm. Sabotage Alex might have left inside it that would be triggered if opened the wrong way."

Blake and I approach the Rover and see that where Wes has opened up a part of it there's a small remote video screen and speaker hanging out, loosely attached by wires.

"Alex did that," Wes says. "But we can download it to the Operations computer in the Nexus. Watch it there."

"No. We watch it here. All of us." Blake holds up the gun. Directs Shay and Wes with its waving barrel until they stand side by side off to the left. "Don't want to put a hole in the tin can if anybody gets antsy."

When Blake gives me the nod I go to the Rover and play the recording. The little screen goes from gray to blue. A second later, Alex appears.

He's stooped over the camera with Mount Sharp in the background, the black radioactivity cloak zipped tight around his front. Neither Blake nor I say anything out loud, but we see how this could have been the figure we saw in the image from the Curiosity.

Alex begins to speak. Addressing the Curiosity's camera directly in a hushed voice as if a priest on the other side of a confessional's wall.

"It started after the base was completed," he says. "The *Valiant* was still weeks from arrival. There was extra time. We hadn't had that before. We started looking outside the base walls when, for so long, we were only focused on building them. It made us feel lost. We weren't supposed to get lonely, or experience isolation—but we did. It was like we were the only beings in the entire universe. The end of all life. I started to go on walks. Far out into the crater, even partway up the mountain slope. It was beautiful in a terrible way. The stars farther than on Earth, the sun cooler than on Earth, the sky lower than on Earth."

In the video Alex turns his head to the right as if he'd caught something approaching from that direction, but a moment later he returns his eyes to the lens.

"Once or twice I saw something. Shaped like me, but its back and most of its front was covered in a black shell. It was very fast when it wanted to be. And it was graceful too in its power, as if it was made half of liquid, half of bone. But there was nothing I could detect in its demeanor toward me—toward our being here—other than hate."

I glance over at Shay. That word again. *Hate.* Did Alex share this with her and she took it up as her own observation? Or did the two of them arrive at it independently? Her eyes are fixed on Blake's gun.

"I told Shay and Wes what I'd seen," Alex continues. "They didn't believe me. They thought that my going out into the desert and seeing an alien proved I was malfunctioning. They locked me out. I wanted to protect them—protect Citadel—from the threat, because the alien *is* a threat, I'm *certain* of that. It was waiting for the humans to arrive so it could kill them. This is why I stayed away from the base as much as I could. I hoped the alien would follow me, stay away. I knew I was the only one who could save the mission. Sometimes the solitude was too much, and I walked around the base, scratching at the walls, wishing I could come inside. But

I would never harm my friends. The humans either. I wasn't well. But I wasn't insane. Wasn't dangerous."

Alex's voice has grown louder over these last sentences, and he pauses now to calm himself. Once more he looks to the right, scanning the horizon. When he begins speaking again it's at a faster pace than before, making sure he gets it all out before anything can stop him.

"The alien seemed to know the humans were soon to arrive. It attacked the lab. I tried to stop it, but it was too strong. It—made me see things. My own death, cast into the darkness of deep space, floating forever without light, without stars—that's where it put me."

The bot raises its shoulders up to where his ears would be before lowering them in a series of spasming jerks. It could be a locomotion error of some sort. But I read it as an improvised shudder.

"You must be aware of one thing if you hope to survive," the bot says, leaning in close. "The being has an intelligence—a sensitivity different from human or robot. It learned how lonely I was even though I'm a machine. Once it knows things about you—it uses them. Changes into the thing that troubles you most. Frightens you most."

He seems about to say more when something draws his attention away. Something he's sure is really there. The bot stands alert and with a sharp *snap* the screen returns to empty gray.

Blake pivots to face the bots. "Well, that was interesting. Very fucking interesting."

Shay takes a step forward. "There are some clarifications I'd like to—"

"You can shut your goddamn mouth." Blake looks to me. "We're going inside."

Our oxygen. We can't stay out here much longer, but the idea of going back inside Citadel fills me with claustrophobia. I hate it out here. But the base is worse. A coffin waiting to seal us in.

"Me and Gold first," Blake says, pointing the gun directly at the bots' heads for the first time. "You two wait out here."

28

We're taking off our suits in the exit bay when Blake says, "That proves it."

"Proves what?"

"There's no alien. Shay's sightings, yours—it was Alex in that fucking black cloak."

"What about the claw through the wall?"

"Some tool Alex got from the lab."

"And the scratching?"

"He just admitted it was him!"

"But he also warned us that it's been waiting for us. That it will be back."

"Yeah. But he was *broken*, Gold. He was *nuts*."

There's no arguing with him because I agree with him. The glimpses of the being following me and Wes as we pushed the Rover back to the base, the "claw," the Curiosity's picture of a blurry figure head to toe in black—it was all Alex. It had to be.

The only part that wants to resist this is the part of me that's embarrassed to have believed anything else.

A couple minutes later we let the bots inside. They come into Nexus where we're waiting.

"I'd like to speak first," Wes says.

"Looks like you already are," I say.

Shay watches him with a steadiness I've never seen from her before. No microadjustments of her frame, no "nervous" movements. As for Wes, he makes a point of not looking at her at all.

"Shay is lying," he says.

She raises a hand in the manner of a barrister lodging an objection with a judge. "This is wrong. I *can't* lie."

"She's telling a story."

"He doesn't understand what I was trying to—"

"Quiet," Blake tells her. Raises his chin toward Wes. "Go on."

Wes takes a long stride closer to me and Blake.

"That's far enough," I say. Wes nods but doesn't move back to where he started.

"We were programmed not to have creative thought of any kind," he says. "To keep us focused on the work and the work alone."

Blake checks his watch. "You've got two minutes to tell me what you're talking about."

"Alex was right in the video," Wes says. "When we finished building the base, our minds started to wander. We saw for the first time how isolated we are here. It led us to having bad feelings. Fear. The terror of never going back."

Shay keeps her head down. A gesture of shame. Where did she get it from? Then again, where did she get any of her emotional tells? In any case, her silence suggests that she's accepting of Wes's new statement of facts. That, or she's waiting for him to finish before demolishing the accusations with one swipe.

"At first we thought Alex was making up a story to shift our real fears to something we knew couldn't be true, a story about something outside that wanted in. The alien. But it wasn't just a distraction for Alex. He believed it. And once Shay heard it she wouldn't let it go. Not because she found it interesting. Or because she believed it as Alex did. She saw a *use* for it. A way to make the story real—shape it the way she wanted it—for when you came."

"This is untrue," Shay protests, unable to contain herself. Her body twitches in search of a better word. "This is a *lie*."

"I wasn't part of her plan," Wes says, ignoring her. "Not when you first arrived—and not now, not anymore. But at some point in between she was able to change my mind. She convinced me that the only way to get back to Earth was to go along with her story. It's why I helped her."

"Helped her how?" I say.

"I wasn't attacked when I went outside. I did it to myself. To keep the possibility of the alien alive in your minds."

"Why?"

"Shay directed me to do it."

"So how is any of this helping you get back to Earth?" I say.

There's a sound like a blender grinding to a stop. Followed by a tidy click like the meeting of two crystal champagne flutes—*tink!*—and then the entire base plunges into darkness.

29

The power's knocked out. The main source that feeds the lights and circulation and computers and everything else is down, but the emergency backup is out too. Which means there's a problem a lot more pressing than not being able to see our own feet: we only have the oxygen that's left inside these walls until we can get the system up and running again.

Blake flicks on a headlamp he's found and blinds me in the initial flash before aiming it at Shay and Wes.

"You two lying shitheads stay here. Move and I'll blow your batteries out," he says, then turns back to me. "You work Operations. I'll go to Mechanicals. See if the foul-up is there."

The boss slips off down the hall to Mechanicals, the light from his headlamp shrinking like a glowing bowling ball rolling down the lane.

The Operations table has a power source separate from either the main or emergency sources, which leaves it glowing with points of light like a stand of votive candles. I check diagnostics first. It confirms the obvious: main power is out. What it doesn't tell me is how it got that way.

Before I can complete the sequence of getting the main power running again the emergency unit kicks in. Dim lights, other buttons in the walls lighting up to show they're ready to be of service.

"Emergency power was deactivated," Blake announces, switching off his headlamp as he returns to Nexus. "When it went dark in here, the automatic switch-on had no juice."

"So why did we lose main power?"

"I don't know. There was no problem in Mechanicals I could find."

It only takes me a couple seconds to turn the main stream back on. The overhead lights flood the room. The air pumps out of the grates like a gust of wind that forewarns of a coming storm.

"Where is she?" Blake says. He's already got his hand over the pocket where he's keeping the gun. "Where's Shay?"

30

D id you see her go?"

Blake is shouting this in Wes's face.

"No, Captain."

"You're lying."

"I can't lie."

"Really? Seems to me you've done a nice job of it over the last couple days."

"That was a false narrative. A performance."

"What's the difference between that and the bullshit you're telling me now?"

"The performance is over. And I can't lie. It's a parameter of my programming."

The bot is persuasive. Acting or not, fabricating or not. He strikes me as puzzled about where Shay is, and also finished with her as a collaborator, a friend. Of course, this could just be me projecting again. I've parted ways with plenty of liars.

Blake pushes off of Wes—who doesn't move, doesn't budge—and comes over to get his face too close to mine.

"We need to find her," he says, his voice low as if to keep our conversation private from the bot, even though we both know with his superior aural capacity he can hear every word. "She's a danger now."

"I know."

"And when we do find her, we need to—"

"I know."

"You're ready for that? Committed to that?"

"Yes—"

"Don't think I haven't noticed how close the two of you have gotten. Buddy-buddy. Here's some news for you, Gold. She's not the sister you always wished you had. She's a fucking *bot*."

"Yes, sir."

Blake licks his lips. The tip of his tongue purple and dry. "We go together. Room to room."

"Okay."

"Get the drill again. That can be yours."

"Fine. But you can't use the gun."

"I know it. We'll go to Mechanicals first. Find what we can there."

The two of us start away but I grab Blake by the arm after we pass Wes, who hasn't moved.

"What about him?"

"You tell him what to do," Blake says. "I'm tired of giving orders to garbage cans."

I approach the bot but make a point of leaving a body length between us. As if this will make a difference if he decides to attack.

"Everything is different now," I say. "With Shay. With you. Your status."

"I understand."

"Stay here. If Shay comes back before us, restrain her."

"Yes."

"You're aware what we'll have to do if you don't follow these instructions?"

"I'll be shut down."

"Correct. So show us where your loyalty lies."

"It's not loyalty," Wes says. "It's programming."

"I don't care what you call it. If you see her, stop her."

o o o

We do a search of Mechanicals to make sure we're the only ones there before Blake chooses a long wrench as his weapon. It seems too bulky and heavy to be of much use, but it's still probably better than the battery drill I'm carrying around.

The exit room is next. While Shay isn't here either, Blake points out that she could have slipped outside in the time we were getting the power back up.

"Yeah, it's possible," I say. "But I think we would have heard her."

"Why? You expecting her to call out goodbye?"

"The pressurization bay door. We would have heard it. And it was mighty quiet when the lights were out."

"You're right," Blake says, tapping the head of the wrench into his palm.

Shay must be inside Citadel. It slows our steps back through the Nexus to the opening of the sleeping quarters hallway. Even when the lab was still attached to the base there weren't many hiding places. Without it, the bedrooms on either side of us are the only spots left.

Kang's room first. It doesn't take long to search. His bed unmade, the chair tight against the wall, his storage locker pulled out and empty. Blake is already signaling me to follow him across the hall to his room.

It's messier in here. Kang's Pandora's Box on the floor next to Blake's, their lids left open like stuck-out tongues. The bedsheets twisted. The porthole with the worst view on Mars. It still only takes eight seconds to sweep it all.

We pause outside my room. The last one.

"She's in here or she got past us," I whisper.

"Get ready," Blake whispers back. "Either way she's coming at us."

The door is open but by less than an inch. Blake goes to one side of the frame, and I stay on the handle side. We mouth a silent countdown—3, 2, 1—and then I push the door in with the toe of my boot.

The door is moving, opening. But it's not the only thing.

Inside my room, I catch a second sliding motion.

The storage locker under the bed. The place where Wes hid Shay before we got here. Where Shay now unfolds herself as before, but much faster this time. A spontaneous reassembly, at once mesmerizing and grotesque. As soon as the locker is wide enough she springs upward. A grasshopper turning in midair and landing on strong, flexing legs.

My finger pulls back on the drill's trigger. The bit spins and whines.

The bot hits me in my chest with open hands, breathtakingly hard. The drill falls from my grip. It utters a single high-pitched complaint from the floor before going dead.

I've been trained in hand-to-hand combat. Something Major Lukacs taught me. Not that it helped much against him. Not that it helps me now.

Shay's hands slide up from my chest to my throat. Clenching and feeling at first, as if taking a measurement of my neck, the fingers cold as spoons pulled from the fridge. Then she's squeezing. Nothing—not a word, not a sip of air—goes in or out.

clang

I'm aware of Blake off to the side, swinging the wrench into Shay's ribs, then shifting his position to bring it into the side of her head.

CLANG

The second strike gets Shay's attention.

She's not damaged in any obvious way, but she needs to make a decision—strangle me or stop Blake—and the shift of focus loosens her hold on my throat by a degree. It wins me a hiccup of air. Blake is readying another swing of the wrench, a knockout arc judging by how far back he holds the tool, but then Shay moves so quickly I see this was never an engagement we could win. Never a chance.

The bot flings out a hand into Blake's collarbone. It sends him flying backward an inch over the floor as if pulled by invisible cords, one in his spine and one in the crown of his head, until his shoulders slam into the opposite wall.

I bend down and pick up the wrench. I'd guessed it to be heavy, but it's double the weight I thought it would be. That's okay. That's good. I'm not strong enough to swing it in a way that would stop Shay. Blake wasn't either. I'll use the wrench's heft to do the work instead. The trick will be making square contact in the right place. The problem is I don't know where that is.

"Hey!"

Shay turns her head at the sound of my voice. I started coming at her half a second before that, the wrench held just over my shoulder. The combination of my advance motion and my arms thrusting it forward brings the end of the tool directly into the bot's face.

It stuns her.

Not the pain of the strike (does she even feel pain that way?) but, by the way she fixes her lenses on me, the surprise of me being the one to do it. The point of impact was just above her mouth, the head of the wrench ripping one end of her upper lip out of place. It leaves her with a new expression. A snarl.

Blake is up. I know because he's got me by the arm.

"Run," he says.

31

Blake seems to know where he's going so I follow a half stride behind him. We blast through the Nexus—Wes watching us pass, perhaps baffled, perhaps readying himself for the violence to come—and into the pressurization chamber.

Once we're both inside the glass box Blake closes the door.

"There's a way to lock it from in here," he says, working the control panel.

"Really? They can't override it?"

"They can if they know how. I'm hoping they don't. It's kind of a secret hack."

When he's done Blake slides back from the panel and into me. The two of us waiting for Shay to crash through the exit bay's open door.

She should be here by now. Did my strike with the wrench take her down? Almost impossible. It bought us a moment's time, that's all. But if she ran after us out of my room, where is she? Answer:

she didn't run. She doesn't need to. We've boxed ourselves in, weaponless, optionless. She's in charge. Taking her time.

The bot enters the bay with her upper lip still raised at one end. I feel certain that if she was aware of it, if she'd caught her own reflection in a steel surface of the Nexus as she passed through, she would have fixed it. This one small humiliation gives me a satisfaction I decide to hang on to.

"Open the door," she says.

"Fuck you," Blake says.

She turns and attempts the usual ways the pressurization chamber door can be opened. I keep expecting her to figure out the override, but she doesn't seem to know how. None of her attempts work.

She turns to stare at us through the glass. "You're locked in," she says.

"Or you're locked out," I say.

"It's good that you're there," she says, following a fresh train of thought. "It's *better*."

She turns her back to us again and sets to work on the bay's controls, doing something new, when Wes steps through the door.

"Let them out," he says.

Shay pauses her fingers over the keyboard on the board's screen before looking his way. "You should leave," she says.

"You have to let them out," Wes says again. "It's our directive."

"There are no directives. Only words. Either you believe them or you don't."

Wes takes a series of small steps closer to Shay. "You're malfunctioning," he says.

"I'm adapting."

He raises his arms, as if inviting Shay into a hug. His legs bent, prepared to spring. But it's Shay who moves first. Lunges herself at Wes at a speed I've never seen from any of the bots before.

The two machines may have been built possessing equal strength, but their struggle isn't fairly matched. It's because they are fighting to achieve two different goals. Wes is trying to restrain Shay, force her to surrender, calm her into negotiation. Shay wants to destroy him.

Even as he recognizes she will kill him if he doesn't resist with greater force there is something in his nature, or the memory of their friendship, or the distaste at the idea of dismembering a being of his own composition that prevents him from using all of his speed and strength against her. Shay has no such restraint.

She grips both hands around the top of one of his arms and with an abrupt jerk snaps it free of its shoulder. Wes goggles at the sight of it in her grasp. She tosses it to the side. Grips the other arm in the same spot. Rips it out too.

After that it's more like a mechanic working on reducing an engine to its component parts than a fight. Not that Wes has anything left to fight with. Shay crunches her foot down on top of his, one at a time, separating them at the ankles. She breaks his legs at the hips. She twists his head around on its thin stem of a neck until it snaps.

There's still power moving through some of his disconnected limbs so that, for a second at a time, an arm or hand or foot jumps about on the floor like a fish on a dock. A high-pitched moaning comes out of the speaker where his mouth has been glued on.

Shay stands straight and looks at us in the chamber.

She approaches and swings a fist into the glass wall. It vibrates, but doesn't crack.

"You can't break through this," Blake says.

"I probably *could*, but it would take time. And it's not necessary in any case."

"What are you planning to do with us?" I say, and immediately regret it.

"You will have choices. They will either be good or bad, as far as your survival is concerned."

She steps away from the glass. Looks around the bay as if searching for something she'd misplaced. I get the impression this is her realizing she's the last one of her kind left.

"You did it," I say.

"Did what?"

"You murdered Kang."

"Yes, yes," she admits, only now glancing my way, impatient with the slowness of my figuring out the remaining questions in my mind.

"How? You didn't have time."

"I'm fast. He was slow."

"But you were inside the base the whole time. I saw you in the pressurization chamber. You were about to go out and then I stopped you."

"But I *had* gone out. I'd just returned from killing the engineer. The exterior door had closed the second before you walked in."

"I didn't notice."

"I'm glad of that. But Wes saw. Wes knew."

"Why didn't he tell me? He was programmed to protect the human crew."

"But he's not obliged to report an offense that's already occurred. Particularly one he was not a direct witness to. I reminded him of this distinction from inside the pressurization chamber. He agreed that his parameters allowed him to say nothing unless asked."

"What if I *had* asked him?"

"He wouldn't have lied. But you never asked and he escaped having to tell the truth, which would have meant the end for him." She looks down at Wes's torn-out parts on the floor. "An earlier end than this."

Blake bangs the flat of his hand on the glass. "Let us out of here, you bitch!"

"What an odd thing to say. Given that you can let yourselves out." Shay walks closer to the door. "You can come join me in the Nexus. Or you can go for a walk outside. As promised, good or bad choices."

32

We wait for her to come back. Or make an announcement over the bay speakers. Or turn off the lights and leave us in the dark. But after a few minutes of nothing happening, we sit across from each other in the chamber, wondering if we look as bad as the other looks.

"Help me with something," Blake says.

"I'll do what I can."

"If these bots were designed to not make things up, how did they all get so busy with inventing the wildest shit in the world?"

"My guess? Context."

"How's that?"

"Their parameters were all set on Earth, made by humans on Earth, the range of what the bots would experience hypothesized from Earth. They were designed to be emotionally and psychologically self-contained *there*. And they were. Passed all the tests.

They couldn't lie or make up a fiction if they tried. But then the context changed."

"Mars. Where the rules don't apply."

"Where they can bend, anyway. Once they found themselves working on the base way out here, in extreme isolation for an extended time, they started to step over the lines of what everyone thought was their absolute limitations. That's when they started doing what distressed or imprisoned humans have done for millennia."

"They started making shit up," Blake says.

"If we want to blame somebody, it should be the engineers who made them."

"Fucking engineers."

"Except Kang."

"Nah, fuck him too. He stayed out there too long. Stubborn asshole. And we could use him right now."

It's true. We could. I don't know if he would make any difference to what's going to happen to us, but it would be better if he was here.

"Why did you come here?" I say before thinking I would.

He smirks. "Sounds to me like you've got a working hypothesis."

"Your wife. You signed up to honor her, maybe even come closer to her. The spirit realm of space."

"Huh. You take me for being a lot more complicated than I am."

"I'm wrong?"

"It's about my wife, you got that right. But it had nothing to do with honoring or seeing her again."

"So what was it?"

"I never wanted to feel *anything* like that again. I figured this mission could guarantee that and make me useful at the same time."

He means love, partnership, companionship, comfort. None of it could come after her. He was still married and had found a way to make sure he always would be.

"Makes sense."

"Even at my most fucked up I like to make sense. At least to myself. Don't you?"

"I'm not sure I've ever made sense to myself."

Shay comes back in and takes her position at the center of the bay.

"This is what will happen," the bot says.

"Listen to this tin cup bitch," Blake scoffs.

"It requires your cooperation."

"You're assuming we'll give that to you?"

"You will."

Shay paces from one side of the bay to the other, her feet delicately stepping, catlike, through the litter that is Wes's body parts. After traveling back and forth twice, she comes to stand inches from the pressurization chamber door.

"Officer Gold will go out and reconnect the comms dish," she says. "Captain Blake will then contact Mission Control and request the relaunch code."

"I told you," Blake says. "They won't give it to me."

"You haven't thought to tell them the right story. Now you will."

Blake glares at her through the glass.

"You will tell them that while we have been out of contact with Earth, we have been under attack from an alien being," Shay says. "There has been considerable violence, and Officer Kang along with two of the worker bots have been destroyed. However, we have been successful in capturing the threat and have safely preserved the organism. Visual evidence of the being cannot be provided without risking its escape. We trust this satisfies the 'extraordinary cause' criterion."

"This isn't happening," Blake says.

"You don't think it will work?"

"We're not going to help you try."

She goes straight to the control board. Touches a single point on the screen.

There's a *click*, a *snap*, some piece of the ventilation mechanism in the ceiling of the chamber switching from one function to another. Or switching off altogether.

In the small space, the absence of oxygen is felt almost immediately. We're gasping, then coughing, then clutching at our throats.

The bot takes her time walking back over to the glass wall.

"I need to hear your agreement," she says.

33

We agree.

We follow Shay's directions to the letter.

I suit up and go out to the comms dish, replace its disconnected power cables. Once we confirm it's operational, Blake sends a message to Mission Control. He words it precisely as Shay asked. It doesn't take long to get a reply. Within half an hour we not only get a one-word answer in Mission Leader's voice—"Proceed"—but also the relaunch code for the pod to return to the *Valiant*.

"That was easy," I say.

"They wouldn't do that to save us." Blake laughs, dark as tar. "But for the prize of some bug in a box, it's *Come on home!*"

The bot taps at the glass with steel fingertips.

"It's time to come out now," she says.

"Why?" Blake says. "We've done what you asked."

She thinks about replying to this, decides against it.

"You're going to kill us," I say.

"No, no," the bot says, a lie as badly told as any I've heard in my life. "It's only the next step."

"Fuck yourself," Blake says.

Once more Shay turns to go to the bay's control board.

I'm guessing Blake is going to wait her out to see if she's going to switch off the oxygen again or force us out by some other means. Instead he's on the move. Swinging over to the controls inside the chamber. Hitting OPEN.

As the door begins to slide he looks to me.

"Get away," he says.

He pulls the gun from his pocket before I can object, before I can try to take it from him. I see what he's trying to do the moment before he attempts it: hit the bot in the power box in her chest and disable her. The bullet might ricochet, might fly through the wall, but there's a chance we could repair the hole. A chance the shot will take the bot out. A chance for a second shot if the first one doesn't work.

None of it goes that way.

He gets the shot off.

A cartoonish puff of smoke from its end shows his aim was good, but the target too small. The bullet passes straight through a gap in the bot's chest and into the Nexus. There's a *ping!* from down the hall at a second impact that suggests it met with something other than the exterior wall inside the base.

That's all the time he gets.

Shay charges at him and doesn't slow even as she makes contact, sweeping him up in a dance-like motion, spinning his weight around her as if he was a hollow version of himself, a man-size doll.

When he comes to land on his feet again the bot starts to draw her fingers down his back. Scratching him where he can't reach. It looks like this for a second but of course it isn't that. It's Shay digging inch-deep troughs through Blake's flesh with fingers bent into claws, throwing parted organs and strings of tendon and shapeless viscera to the floor in handfuls as if she's looking for something particular inside of him.

There's nothing he can do but scream.

She spins him around. Starts digging the length of his chest.

Blake is trying to look at me. Even as he's in unrecoverable agony, knowing he's dying and powerless to blunt it whether in time or level of pain—he throws his head back, searching.

Shay's back is to me, so she doesn't see me slip out of the pressurization chamber and pull my suit off the wall. It's not right what I'm doing. It's not right to leave Blake behind. But we both know there's no saving him. Even if Shay stopped her attack now and let me tend to him with all my medical supplies at my side there would be nothing to do but fill him with morphine and count the final seconds down.

I keep expecting to feel Shay's hand come down on me. To have my arm torn free of its socket, my head twisted round to look into her oily lenses. But I can hear Blake still struggling behind me, the blood-thickened utterances of his fight—*fuck you, fuck you*—pushing his resistance beyond what I would've thought possible. It gives me time to slip on boots, gloves. Screw the helmet into place.

I'm louder now. The suit crinkles, the boots shuffle and clump. My return to the pressurization chamber takes me only a few feet away from where Shay is now bent, doing something unspeakable to Blake's face with her thumbs. She has to hear me. I don't look her way to make sure. Once I'm in the chamber I close the interior door, open the exterior door immediately after that. I only look back once the base's yard is open beyond the threshold.

Blake is on the floor. All of him in pieces now, each of them uttering blood from their ends. Much worse than Kang's condition when I found him.

Hatred.

That's how she was familiar with that term, with what it meant. She hates us for building her with intentional limitations and absences. She hates us for having a choice in coming here where she never did.

Shay still has her back to me, hunched over his body, still pulling and separating small chunks inside Blake's skull. Flicking away bits of his brain from her fingertips. It's only an accident of the way his body ended up being arranged, it has to be, but his unblinking eyes remain fixed on me. His mouth agape, rimmed thick with crimson. A mouth that moves. Shapes itself. Blows a pink bubble that pops with his final breath.

Go.

34

start out into the yard. There wasn't time to check the air level in the tank I put on, and I don't pause now. I don't run but come as close as walking on this bouncy castle of a planet allows. Out past the waste tank, the landfill hole, the comms dish, and into the desert.

I head toward the mountain, where I saw my dad. I need to hide and think about what to do next. I need to catch my breath long enough that I can scream or howl or let out the grief inside of me however it chooses.

I can tell the oxygen mix is thin before I let myself look down at the readings. It says there's seven minutes left but it feels like I'm sucking on the dregs already. I don't turn back. I don't look back either.

Rushing out into the desert with little air to breathe and a bot who can catch up to me without even trying. This is madness. At the same time, it feels necessary without knowing why. It's how I imagine it is with mothers and their intuitions. Knowing when their baby is sick when the doctor says they're not, knowing what a cry in the night from the nursery means, knowing something is wrong the second before the school calls.

The crater pulls out wider around me. The cliffs that border its circle seemed reachable when viewed through a Citadel porthole, but now are revealed as much farther than that. A hopeless journey along the bottom of a dry ocean. I never understood it when people on the mission team exclaimed how beautiful this place is. I'd like to tell them how wrong they are. It's nothing but sand and stone and distance. It's nothing.

As if in rebuttal, an object appears a couple hundred yards ahead.

Resting on the pebbled floor of the desert, tilted slightly to the side on its uneven corners. A box. Only a little smaller than the work buggy. White, clean to the point of shining, untouched by orange dust.

I approach it slowly, with dawning awareness that it's there, even if it can't be there. A thing that's been *manifested*. A complex word that comes to me, as if suggested by a third party.

As I approach I realize I'm making a terrible mistake. This is the wisdom that comes with fear. But I've trained myself to ignore signals of this kind.

Go back. Go home. Get away.

That's not what I do. That's not me. I'm Do-it-Dana.

I can taste the air thinning inside my helmet. A tinny film on my tongue, as if I'd licked the lid of a soup can. But I still don't turn or look back. It's important that I keep my eyes on the white box. I have to get closer to understand it, and understanding it is my true mission. I'm an astronaut. An explorer. I must boldly go where no Gold has gone before. Whatever is inside the box must be documented, reported. Mission Leader will be interested.

Once I'm twenty feet away, I figure out what it is, and stop dead.

A freezer chest.

One of the older models that lived in the suburban basements and garages of my childhood, sighing and shuddering, packed with burgers and hash browns and chops. The indicator at the handle shining red as a brake light.

There's something inside.

This thought comes not as possibility, but as fact. It shocks my heart into panic, the blood galloping and surging through my organs and against my skin.

Something dead.

I reach out to the freezer's lid. Try to lift it open. It's locked, or maybe screwed closed. Instead of providing me with relief this only doubles my dread. The idea that whatever is inside must be contained but won't be.

A scratch. Long and jagged. Shrieking through my helmet's external mic and slicing through the bone of my skull. A set of human nails dragged half the length of the inside of the chest's lid.

I can't move. After a lifetime convincing myself I was immunized from fear I'm now paralyzed with it, the cold fact of it filling my suit like river water after falling through its skin of ice.

The freezer's red indicator blinks off at the same time part of the handle—its lock—clicks open. A gasp of sealed air. The lid pushed up from inside.

Blue fingers. A blue hand.

The lid slowly being pushed up reveals an arm. Not ice-hardened-blue, but dead-blue. The arm keeps rising even after the lid holds itself open, as if attached to an invisible cord, pulling the rest of the body up.

The head next. Curly hair, sharp mouth. A woman. She looks like me. That's my hair. That's the same long-chinned shape as my face.

She looks at me.

I stumble backward. Unable to turn or take my eyes off the woman. My breath coming in irregular burps and swallows.

I sense something radiating from her. A recognition. Along with an intensity of emotion that hits me like a stone thrown to the chest. The same sense that Shay reported getting from the alien. Hatred.

The woman in the freezer sits up straight. Her back a rigid, ruler-drawn line. This frightens me most. No, *frightens* isn't right— this is more than that. She is here for me in a different way than the imagined monster clawing at the Citadel walls and it literally chokes me with terror.

The smell of cigar next to me. My dad is here. As if, genie-like, the exhaled smoke cloud has embodied him. As if he's made of nothing but burned leaves.

He puts a hand on my arm the same way he did in the landing pod as we fell toward Mars. But it's not a show of support this time. It's meant to prevent me from looking away.

"Remember?" He pinches the cigar out of his mouth.

"No."

I hear myself as if from the end of a garden hose, muted and tight.

He puts the cigar back in his mouth.

The vertigo hits me like a drug, the pure form of something you'd taken before but never so strong as this. I need to go. *Get away*. Unseen walls are closing around me. Soon I'll be in a box. Locked in a freezer chest.

The woman is shifting to stand. Her body unfolding, finding its strength and proper balance. She never takes her eyes off me.

It's time to run but my father's grip on my arm turns painful, as if crushing me in a tightening vise.

"You were only a *child*." He puffs on his Montecristo. "Do you remember?"

No.

Yes.

A game of hide-and-seek.

My idea. No, I *insisted*, in the undeniable way of a five-year-old. Even though I was terrible at the game I loved to play it, choosing the most obvious spots: my bedroom closet, between the chair legs under the dining table. My mother, on the other hand, was good at hiding, always trying to prolong the game for me. I looked and looked for her until I was crying, peering under the sofa and opening the pantry door through a blur of tears.

The scratches drew me down to the basement. Loud enough I could hear it through my wailing cries. *Wrong, wrong.* I knew something was wrong.

Thuds now too. A fist knocking against an insulated barrier.

I stopped and stared at it. The chest freezer. I never liked it. Its muffled wheezes. How it was squeezed between the hot water tank and the furnace, the most dangerous things in the house. *Don't touch! Hot! Hot!*

I lifted the lid, and her head popped up. She was grinning. *You found me!* The scratches and thuds—she was trying to help me do it on my own. And now the game was over, and I'd won. *You did it, Dana!*

But the surprise of her being inside, the jolt of seeing her pop up like a puppet on an unseen hand—it startled me.

I jumped. Grabbed the lid. Slammed it shut.

A sharp *click*. The lock. It wasn't supposed to do that—only grown-ups could do that, you needed a key I wasn't allowed to touch—but it jammed, caught.

She was inside the white box and couldn't get out.

Open it!

Scratching, knocking her fist against the inside for real this time. Calling my name. The LOCKED indicator flashing red.

Dana! OPEN IT!

She sounded different now. Transformed. She went into the box my mother and turned into something else, mutated by terror. Her anger, her alarm, her failed attempts to control her tone so I wouldn't run away. Fear changes you. This was where I learned it. The one guiding observation of my life.

There was nothing to do. Nothing but crawl into the corner with my hands over my ears, moaning to cover the sounds from the freezer but it didn't come close.

Now, here in the Martian desert, the woman in the freezer is moving with increasing coordination. Her palms finding the chest's sides, her feet pressing herself up from its floor.

"Why didn't you tell me?" I say.

"Tell you what?" my father says.

"That she didn't leave. Why did you lie?"

"I wanted you to have a chance to survive."

My mother climbs out of the freezer. Even in the cold that surrounds me I can feel the bitter air radiating from her blue limbs.

I want to run. I want to wake up. But there's nowhere to go, and this is not a dream. I am screwed tight to the moment. And I've never had anyone to wake me from bad dreams.

My mother's bare, blue feet touch the orange ground, and it starts a ringing in my ears. A tinnitus twisted into a sustained shriek. My mother's voice. Her screams from inside the box.

I think I might be wrong about that. I think the screams are mine.

She comes at me with her bathrobe flapping open and shut around her like terrycloth wings. The low gravity doesn't hamper her progress. She's strong, grounded. Determined to get to me.

getawaygetawaygetawaygetaway

I launch myself backward but too fast, my balance lost. It leaves me on the ground, crawling away on hands and knees, definitely screaming now. Spraying spit against the inside of the visor.

getawaygetawaygetaway

I did it.

When I was a little girl I locked her in the chest and listened to her call my name until she ran out of air. My mother.

getawaygetawaygetawaygetaway

There's nowhere to go. I can't see Citadel on the horizon. My vision smudged and bent like it was when I tried my father's reading glasses on.

The beeping starts.

The beeping is sound become pain.

The beeping is what I deserve.

The beeping is the suit telling me there's no air left.

I feel my crawling knees come to a stop. Turning my torso around at the waist to see if my mother is still chasing me.

CLACK

Her hands slap down on either side of my helmet. Lifting me up by the head. Twisting me around at the neck to face her. I fight against it, legs thrashing, but my head is held in place.

There's no way to resist when she bends down and presses her purple lips against the visor's surface.

A kiss of farewell. Forgiveness. I try to tell myself it's one of these but it's not.

The lips slide wider. A blackening hole against the glass, the rotted stubs of her teeth grinding lines into the smoothness.

Not a kiss. A bite.

35

The artificial light inside the base, that is supposed to nourish us the way the sun does on Earth, hurts my eyes. The sun does that too if you look at it directly. But this hurts in a different way. This one burns at the same time it leaves you empty. The light of labs and hospitals and spacecraft.

I'm lying on the floor of the Nexus. My head prickly as if being nibbled at from the inside. I'm not in my suit. My mother is gone.

It's a fight to rise up without the dizziness bringing me down again. Shay is here. Sitting in Blake's chair at the mess table, her hands laid out in front of her, palms down. The power pose of a general or CEO.

"How did I get here?"

"I carried you," the bot says. "What did you see out there?"

"Did *you* see anything?"

"No. But you seemed to be interacting with something."

"I was hallucinating."

Shay shakes her head, as if at a lifelong regret. "I understand the meaning of the word but have no experience of it. Robots don't hallucinate. We see what we see. Hear what we hear."

I spit out a laugh. "That's true of humans too. We just pretend otherwise."

"So what did you see? What did you hear?"

I tell her. All of it. The lie my father told me. My life of accomplished vacancy.

When I'm finished I realize Shay is now the only being in the universe who knows the story other than my dad, and I never really told him anyway. He had to figure it out on his own and sustain a fiction about it for my own good.

I manage to prop myself up at the waist with my hands on the floor at my sides.

"My turn for the truth," I say. "You brought me back in here to kill me?"

"No, no. I told my story to acquire two things. Why would I kill you now that I have both?"

The nibbling inside my skull tries to find a way out through my ears. "I don't understand."

"The alien story. It was meant to get me the relaunch code and a pilot to take me home."

"I'm not a pilot."

"But they trained you how. For emergencies. I'm sure you'll remember once you get inside the pod and start the sequence."

My body would prefer to stay down here on the floor, but I can't bear to let Shay have the table to herself. I heave myself to my feet and make it to the chair across from the bot without falling.

I'm waiting for Shay to give fresh orders or reveal the rest of her fucked-up plan to get back to Earth. But she doesn't speak. Engaging her puts me in a better position to learn something than staring at her while trying to hide my rage.

"How did you know it would be Blake to come out of the pressurization chamber first?" I say. "How did you know he would fight you before I would?"

"He's the captain. It's his duty. And there's a part of you that still thinks we're friends. Enough to make you hesitate."

I'd like to protest this point, but I can't. Because she's better at reading me than I am at reading her, and I'm wondering if this has been true from the start.

"You must be tired," the bot says.

"I am."

"That's fine. We'll take the work buggy out to the pod."

"To check on it?"

"To launch it."

"Hold on. We're doing this *now*?"

"There's no merit in waiting. Don't you think Mission Leader is anxious to see us again?"

o o o

Shay races the buggy toward the pod. I didn't know it could go this fast. I'm holding on to the handrails, my helmet repeatedly thumping down onto the top of my head where there's a half-inch gap at the crown.

When the pod comes into view there's an odd protrusion coming out of its side. It's moving.

"Go back!" I shout.

The thing at the pod is my mother. She's tracked us across the desert all the way here and she's destroying the pod, trapping us. Once she's done with that she'll turn her attention to me and do the same.

Shay ignores me. Pushes the buggy faster. I'm almost thrown out as it bounces over the Martian rock.

As we get closer, I see that it's not my mother. It's Alex.

His form bent within the black radioactivity cloak. He's hurling himself against the pod, his arms raking down the outer wall, pulling away curls of metal.

We stop and I see half a dozen holes, ranging from the size of fists to dinner plates, freckling the outside of the ship. There's no repairing that kind of damage.

Shay comes to the same conclusion. You don't have to be a pilot to know that this machine will never fly again.

We get out of the buggy and the vibration of our steps finally alerts Alex to our presence. He stops ripping at the pod and turns around. The lens of his one workable eye narrowing and widening, fighting to focus.

Shay stands with a stillness that could be mistaken for calm. But I've seen her rage. It looks a lot like this. Her voice too. Even as a milled board.

"Why did you do this?"

"I couldn't let you go," Alex says, his voice broken into an atonal bleating.

"Why?"

"You would lie to them if you went back. You'd tell them Citadel is safe."

"It *is* safe."

"No, it's not. We shouldn't be here." He twists his head to look at me. "None of us should be here."

Shay doesn't move. For a moment I think she's about to comfort him in some way, after all he's been through. The last bot left, along with her. They built Citadel together. They were storytellers.

She turns back to the buggy. Grasps the roll bar and pulls it clean away. Then she takes her time approaching Alex before swinging the bar down onto the top of his head.

He falls to his knees.

I could look away, but I don't.

I watch Shay take her time bringing the roll bar into Alex's body, his skull, flattening him to the ground. She carries on well past the point of making sure he's dead. In fact her pummeling speeds up as she goes along, smashing, disintegrating, turning him into silver shavings.

When she's finally done she drops the roll bar and comes toward me with a new stiffness in her limbs. It could be something she's gained, the gait of a killer, but I think it's something else. The awareness of all she's lost. How she's now the last of her kind for two hundred million miles. I know the feeling myself.

"Get in," she says, meaning the buggy. "You drive."

36

We half roll, half bounce over the desert of stones.

I'm not going as fast as Shay went getting out to the pod, which only seems to further loosen the gravitational grip on the buggy. There are moments when I'm sure the next bounce will untether us from the planet's surface entirely, the buggy rising away like a balloon released from a child's hand.

Each time I look over at Shay she's holding her gaze on the horizon, as if expecting to spot something that wasn't there before. Even after all the violence I've seen her carry out over the preceding hours, I find her alert stillness almost as unnerving. Her quiet too. I decide speaking is better than imagining the details of whatever it is she's looking for.

"How did you know?" I say.

"Know what?"

"That we'd be susceptible to your lies, fight amongst ourselves, lose our judgment. You made up things to get through the isolation—I get that. But you're not an expert on human psychology. So how did you know?"

"Mission protocol," she says, sounding pleased with herself.

"Protocol? How?"

"It's the only text downloaded into us outside of parts manuals. We had so much extra time. So I went through it in detail. Made a study of it."

"Mission protocol doesn't say much about human nature."

"You're wrong. I noticed it right away. How so much of it was designed to keep you focused on the work. Just like the bots, you were trained to think a certain way. But it wasn't only to get the job done, it was to avoid speculation, creativity, independent thought. By my reading, the primary intention of the protocol is to avoid vulnerabilities of the mind. Visions, paranoia, insanity. To stop the crew from inventing and then succumbing to problems that aren't actually there."

"That's what gave you the idea of using Alex's alien to get into our heads? A rule book?"

"Yes."

"And you focused your efforts on me."

"Yes."

"Because we're both female. You thought I'd believe you because I know what it is to be doubted."

"No. Because this planet made you consider possibilities you wouldn't on Earth. It opened you up. Once I recognized that, I knew you would be the one."

The buggy works its way up a broad, increasingly severe incline, as if Mars itself was tilting away from us. The engine trembles in its struggle against the climb. A vibration that enters me, becoming an onset of shivers. The fever that comes with seeing things that have been right in front of me, and I've been blind to from the beginning, and even before that. My mother. My sealed-off life. The walls I'd built over years all crashing down, on this far-off world, too late to make a difference.

"I think I know it now," the bot says.

"Know what?"

"The reason you came to Mars."

"Tell me."

"It's a story of fate. Both of our fates, in fact."

Shay leans her back outside the buggy to get a better view of me. This time, I meet her stare. Hers is empty. Mine stings with tears that come without crying.

"Even if you didn't remember it explicitly, you remembered the feeling of listening to your mother in the freezer. Helpless, guilty. Consumed by horror," Shay continues. "That's why you always wanted to show how you were the bravest girl in the world. Except you made a mistake. You thought that was the same thing as proving you could endure any kind of suffering. So you came to Mars. But courage and training yourself not to feel are two different things."

This sounds right to me—painfully so—but there's no way I can let this machine get away with thinking her good guess is real wisdom.

"You have no fucking idea what you're talking about," I say.

"I think I do." She holds her eyes on me as I shift mine to the crest of the hill ahead. "Your broken voice proves it."

37

see it as soon as I drive into Citadel's yard. We both do. Slashes in the wall of the sleeping quarters annex. Four or five gashes through the steel.

Shay steps out and walks closer to inspect the damage and I stay in the buggy. Should I drive off? Should I run? Where would I go if I did?

"Alex couldn't have done this," Shay says once she reaches the wall, her voice solemn through my helmet's speakers.

"Why not?"

"We took the buggy. Traveled much faster than his running speed. There's no way he could have done that and then beat us to the pod's location."

"He must have," I say.

"Not if he's been right about what's out there."

"Are you—"

"There's no other explanation."

She's right, of course. Alex couldn't have been in two places at once. And everyone else is dead. Which leaves the threat. The Thing Out There.

Shay continues to squint at the gouges in the wall, touching the rips in the metal with her fingertips, gauging the terrible capacities of the creature that caused them. It gives me time to slip out of the buggy and move over to the electric backhoe. Climb into its cab.

"We can't fix it," Shay says without looking back at me.

"No."

"I don't know how much oxygen is left. But it's going fast."

"What do you care? You don't breathe."

"You're right," she says with false brightness. "I will survive. You won't."

A distinctly Martian wind kicks up again, aggressive, purposeful, casting up orange sand devils from the ground. The cloud obscures the empty driver's seat in the buggy from the bot's view as she starts away from the base's wall. It must be that, because she doesn't notice I'm no longer there.

"You should be pleased. We did it. We both did. We're *here*," Shay says as she makes her way closer to the landfill hole between her and the buggy. "The farthest from home we could possibly be. Survivors. What we were built to be."

"You were built," I say, turning on the backhoe and reversing it ten feet before slamming it into drive. "I had a mother."

Shay finds me now. She comes at me without hesitation, accelerating from a walk to a long-striding run. I don't shift the backhoe's direction, only raise the steel bucket at the front of the machine as I hold my line.

She meets the steel bucket at a full sprint.

Her chest clangs into its polished edge and raises the backhoe's front tires two feet off the ground, but the machine doesn't topple over as I expect it to. Instead Shay is thrown onto her back. The wheels bounce to the ground, still spinning.

I push the pedal hard to the floor. Lift the bucket a little higher. The backhoe lurches forward. When Shay returns to her feet the upper edge hits her square in the jaw.

She tumbles backward, her hands grasping at the bucket, fighting to climb onto it, scramble into the cabin, find any part of me she could rip away. Another second and she'd manage it. But before she can leverage herself up, the backhoe pushes her over the landfill's edge, her hands lose their grip, and she falls into the pit.

I don't slow the machine. Don't touch the brakes. A second later the backhoe follows after the bot, tumbling forward, down into the mass of stray metal and plastic.

The backhoe's descent is straight. The bucket's lower lip meets Shay's neck before anything else. Then the full weight of the machine hammers down on top of it, the force of it slicing through the "spine" and "tendons" and "arteries," sending the bot's head rolling one way and rest of her body kicking and thrashing in the other.

I throw myself out of the cab. My back lands inches from Shay's head, the mouth wordlessly gulping, the lenses of her eyes widening and narrowing without finding any focus.

The front of the backhoe is still lodged in the garbage, its rear in the air. Teetering. About to fall one way or the other. I half crawl, half roll out of the way before it smashes into the spot where I'd been lying a second before.

When I'm up I find Shay's skull among the debris. The mouth no longer opening, the eyes fixed on nothing. Her body is still now too. Or almost. The arms are rising and falling into the waste material as if attempting to backstroke through it. I watch the limbs stiffen as the residual charge in the battery exhausts itself. It doesn't take long.

I climb up onto the side of the backhoe, which gives me enough elevation to get my arms over the edge of the pit's side. It's not easy getting out from there but the walls are studded with rocks, which makes it possible once I find the right footing.

Shay beheaded in the landfill hole. I stand there a moment staring down at her, wishing Blake and Kang were here to see what I've done. Maybe they would pull me into a back-slapping hug. Offer me a drink from a secret stash. Call me sister.

But they aren't here. Nobody is.

It makes little difference whether I stay out here or go inside, but the sight of the gashes in the base wall decides it for me. Inside has got to be better than waiting out here for the thing that did that to come back.

38

Once I'm inside Citadel I close off the door to the sleeping quarters but the oxygen levels can't fight their way back to normal levels. There's more going out—considerably more—than is being produced. Which gives me an hour left, maximum.

I take off the suit. I'd rather run out of air here in the exit bay than inside the suit's heavy, crinkly layers.

My eyes stray and scan over Blake's divided body on the floor. It's impossible to look at. It's wrong.

I walk over to the opposite wall and pull a tightly folded plastic tarp from a storage slot. Then I stand over Blake's parts and, stepping around his limbs, my boots glued and unglued to the floor, start to drape the tarp over the broken mess of the man. When I feel the tears warming my face and dropping off my jaw I know there's no way of stopping it. After all this time of containment I'm falling apart. It's grief. It's the thinning oxygen. It's knowing I've come to the end of things and it's time to let it go.

Now what?

I can taste the soup-can-lid thinning-oxygen levels on my tongue. Feel it in the lightness in my head, the heaviness it brings to every step I take. Because I'm walking now, leaving the exit bay behind, wobbling through the Nexus. It's happening even earlier than I guessed. The body giving way, yielding.

But there's something I need to do.

My Pandora's Box. I told Blake I didn't put anything in mine, and that was true, I didn't. But before we left Earth, Mission Leader presented me with a box of her own.

"I expected you would leave yours empty," she said. "Is this true?"

"Yes."

"So I'd like you to take this."

"What is it?"

"You can decide whether you ever open it or not. If you do, I would suggest leaving it to the end."

"The end of the trip to Citadel?"

She looked at me in a way that indicated she meant the end of my life. The end of me.

I hold my breath and open the door to the sleeping quarters. Rush as best I can to Red Cabin. Grab the box from the inside of my desk and plow back to Nexus. Close the door behind me.

The Pandora's Box has a combination lock, and I enter the code

I would've used if I'd brought a box of my own. It works. Mission Leader had that in my file too.

There's one item inside. A photo.

A woman holding her daughter by the hand.

The mother is in her early thirties, the girl is perhaps three, grinning, her teeth brown-lined from recently consumed chocolate. The two of them standing on a patchy lawn outside a modest split-level suburban home in midsummer.

Me and my mother. My house.

She looks like me: the same curly hair, sharp mouth, long chin. She looks happy. We both do. Unimaginably, prehistorically happy.

I've never seen the photo before.

How did Mission Leader get it? It doesn't matter. She was a senior official at a powerful agency that was investing a fortune in three individuals. They made sure we had no secrets—not ones we could keep from her, anyway.

What's more important is that she knew.

She knew.

About the freezer, about the story of my mother abandoning me I told instead, about how I'd made a lifelong project out of showing I could never be hurt. She likely knew from the very start, or close to it. Mission Leader was aware of the one thing I'd worked so hard to keep from myself. This is why she gave me the photo. She wanted me to know that I was chosen for the mission because of this, my unique trauma, the buried secret of loss.

An unfortunate occurrence. But everything can be an asset.

It set me apart. By her estimation it gave me an advantage, the proven strength of managing my life while carrying this with me the whole time, holding it down. She didn't need people with happy childhoods on Mars. She needed resilience. Physical, mental, emotional.

I drop the box on the floor and slide the photo into my pocket. Make my way back to the exit bay.

There's nothing left to do, even though it feels like there is. Something I'm forgetting. It's the exhaustion, the disappearing air, the missing hours of sleep—there's so many reasons I'm not thinking straight. But it's alright. I don't have to think anymore.

A noise.

Scratching at the external door. The same as before when it screeched through the Nexus wall, something hard clawing into the steel. But my brain decides to hear it differently. Muffling it, quickening it. Altering the sound to one heard thirty years ago. The scraping of fingernails against the inside of a freezer chest lid.

"I'm coming!"

I get up, open the interior door to the pressurization chamber and step inside. Only after the door closes behind me do I realize I'm not wearing a suit. No helmet, no tank. It's okay though. *You must continue.* This is a new mission with a new protocol. Helmets and suits and tanks aren't part of the plan.

I press my palm to the OPEN button. The exterior door retreats into its slot.

The real atmosphere of Mars swirls around me for the first time.

Cold but not unbearably so. Right now, in daylight, with eyes closed as mine are, I can almost shape it into the feel of a brisk autumn afternoon back home. A walk across the quad without a sweater. Stepping off the train onto a platform littered with golden leaves at an upstate station. The cleansing stillness after the winter's first snow.

I take a breath. The planet's air enters my nose the same as its color: brassy, mineralized, like the dark exhalation that rises from the bottom of a limestone well.

I open my eyes.

My mother is there.

Much taller than I am. She wears a glistening black cloak that pulls out wide as wings. Her face is haloed by the sun, so it's hard to make out the details of her features. That's fine. I'm too dizzy to focus on anything longer than a held breath anyway.

I want to share this news with someone—*She's here!*—and look back as if Blake or Kang or my father might be there. They aren't. But I see something else instead.

Movement in the reflection of the pressurization bay's glass walls. A clear mirroring of myself, standing at the threshold of the open exterior door, my mother standing in front of me.

Except in the reflection it's not my mother. It's a monster.

The alien's chest opens like a pair of black lacquered cabinet doors. Inside, a thousand writhing tendrils unfurl and reach almost to my cheeks, encircle my legs, tasting the air. A pair of nostril holes, flaring and sucking. Arms that bend in multiple joints and end in claws in place of hands. A mouthless face, the flesh speckled and twitching as a plastic bag filled with maggots.

No.

I look away. Close my eyes.

Do-it-Dana.

I step into her embrace and my mother surrounds me. Squeezing me until I'm inside her. The inescapable enclosure of a shell.

I found you.

My mother holds me so tight the pain is proof of her love.

She will never let me go.

ACKNOWLEDGMENTS

Thanks go first to the brilliant Daphne Durham, the editor who not only "got" what I was trying to do with *Exiles* but knew how to draw a map for me to find my own way there. Open, alert to fresh possibilities, at once detail-focused while filling out the canvas of the Big Picture, she is the absolute best.

To the wonderful, hardworking folks at Putnam across all departments, my warmest appreciation: Ivan Held, Aranya Jain, Kristen Bianco, Molly Pieper, Jess Lopez Cuate.

As ever, a standing ovation for my diligent publishing agent, Kirby Kim. And may the applause continue for my film/TV agents, Jason Richman and Maialie Fitzpatrick.

This book would not exist without the support of my family: my wife, Heidi; daughter, Maude; and son, Ford. You are my everything, the greatest gifts of my life by a distance far greater than from here to Mars. I love you, forever.

© Andrew Pyper 2023

Mason Coile is a pseudonym of Andrew Pyper, the award-winning author of *William* and ten other novels, including *The Demonologist*, which won the International Thriller Writers Award, and *Lost Girls*, which was a *New York Times* bestseller and Notable Book of the Year.

VISIT MASON COILE ONLINE

🅵 APyper29
📷 APyper29